CHIQUITITA

CHIQUITITA

Pedro Carmona-Alvarez

Translated from the Norwegian by
Seán Kinsella

akoya

LONDON

'Tell me I'm pretty, tell me I'm rare
Talk to the boy in me, he's there.'
Adrianne Lenker

'Chiquitita, tell me what's wrong.'
ABBA

1

It starts by the sea. There, is the sea. The day is grey, winter by the look of it. Bitterly cold, a dampness in the air, like in a basement below the ground. A wind blows, in gusts. The reeds on the beach sway, frozen, faded. Are there reeds in winter, or does everything die? I don't know. I can't remember everything. The waves on that side of the lighthouse are treacherous, the father says. You must never swim there. Do you see them, he says, but it's as though he's looking at something other than the waves, the reeds, me. The lighthouse is beautiful. Freshly painted. A sign says not to write, scratch or carve on the wall. A heart. An arrow. *P + EL.* I sit on the wall, dangling my legs. It's not far down. The sand catches me when I jump. It's just a little too high, but I'm a big girl now, so it's OK. The sand is cold, a dampness about it also. In the distance a pack of dogs, thin as partition walls, I think to myself *later later later*, when I replay the scene in my mind's eye. But it's not really a scene. Just a series of things, crumbs on a plastic kitchen table in the grandmother's house. Red tiles. Insignificant things, interchangeable things. And yet, for me. That exact wall. That exact door handle. That exact sound of the man on a big tricycle, a freezer box mounted on the handlebars, calling out that he has ice cream for sale.

This is how you collect. One thing connects to the next. Then gives way to a landslide. But before that, ever so slowly, it builds into a mountain. A mountain of crumbs and dogs, of reeds and tricycles and the father with his back turned talking to me as though talking to himself. The grandmother's white hands. Roasted corn in the pocket of an apron. My life when I was a child.

An ordinary child at first, who is given a name, the mother's choice really: *Marisol.* After the Virgin. And the sun. Both of those things. The father wants me to be called something else, to be named after a female revolutionary, but it's not so important to him so he gives in, and lets the mother choose Marisol. She pats her stomach and speaks to me from her world. I don't remember this but have been told that I once said I did. That I claimed to have felt, to have remembered, a gentle impact, as though the bumper of a car had nudged a garage door.

Once I fell into a river. The water was grey and viscous. I don't know how long I was under. When I came up, the father was standing by a tree looking at me. I've dreamed a lot about that tree. I was dressed in some dry clothes they borrowed. No doubt too big for me. The mother was worked up, shouted at me, her voice simultaneously questioning, accusing and desperate. She was frightened. She shouts when she's frightened. I saw yellow fish under the water. They swam back and forth before my eyes as though they wanted to say: what's this girl doing here, she's not supposed to be here. The grown-ups laughed. There are no fish in the rivers, only in the sea, the mother said, or maybe it was the father. I felt ashamed when they laughed. I couldn't have known that what I'd seen didn't exist. No one had taught me that.

That night I dreamed about a garden. It was crooked, dense and dark, like a Renaissance painting.

I floated by a crooked tree, old and rough. Everything around me was greenish, almost mouldy. The sky was filled with heavy, rolling clouds, leaden. In the dream I thought, now God is going to turn up, now you're going to see God. I was woken by the mother. The bed was wet and I curled up, curled up my voice too.

At night I wet my bed. My bed is yellow, as is the mother's face, and my room, the walls, for evermore. How can that be? I can't sleep afterwards, after I've been dried and the mother has torn open a bin liner, placed it over the mattress and tucked me under a blanket she's fetched from the living room. Tell me you didn't piss on the pillow as well, she says.

The mother is also a daughter, one of several. They're my aunts. There are brothers too, sons, they're called the uncles. I'm the first child, the daughter. I have the same name as the Virgin and the sun. No one wet the bed until I came along. I can't fall asleep at night, I'm scared of pee. But in the daytime, I shine like a sun, the mother says. She clothes me in dresses I love. She holds my hand when we enter the grandmother's house, where I have to sleep, eat, talk to the aunts and uncles, be the niece, the very first child.

Everything I do is new. The winter sun is yellow like the pee stains. How can that be? The grown-ups teach me the names of birds, gods, touch my hair and call me pearl, sweet pearl, daughter, sometimes jewel, sun, my sun, and heart. But I want to be called mist.

No, that's later. Much later. My name is Marisol. *Later* means everything that hasn't happened yet but which will happen. *Later,* I say to myself when I'm alone in a corner, behind a curtain with an abandoned doll. *Later later later,* like a refrain. A sentence I utter with shame because I'm sure it's not mine, not really. I say this: I am only truly alive to myself by the river behind the grandmother's house, where I'm washing a slice of apple, over and over. *Like a raccoon,* a man says to me. More of a boy, really. For a long time, I don't want anything to do with him. I don't respond to his approaches. I don't know what he wants. But he's the type who isn't easily discouraged, who looks at me as though through a crack, who stands at the edges waiting for me. We meet at parties, occasionally. I avoid him. I don't know why. But then. He becomes my first love, the first real one. We're nearly adults by then, *later later later*, when I mention the river to him, the slice of apple, the washing of it, my life.

I'm ashamed so often that I forget it's shame I feel. God doesn't appear in my dream and I'm ashamed for believing He would. I'm ashamed of the yellow fish I saw, of the river I fell into, of my wet clothes and of the dry ones someone had to lend me. I laugh at myself when the grown-ups laugh and I'm ashamed of doing so. Then the mother's face is serious. It's a responsibility, my responsibility. Her brow is furrowed, even though she's young and radiant. I ruined the family outing. The mother was frightened, presumably, frightened that I would drown, be pulled from the river, drowned. She ran around, calling my name, gently at first, warily, as though she didn't actually believe that what had happened had happened. Then her voice grew increasingly stern. I could hear it under the water. Her voice is slower, slower than when she pulled me up and half hugged me, half slapped me. The rest of the afternoon the grown-ups eat big chunks of meat with their hands. Everything has turned out all right. The mother wears sunglasses and prefers not to look my way, is more interested in her cousin, the funny aunt who I don't like, who I'm ashamed of not liking. When it grows chilly, I'm loaned more clothing. The eucalyptus trees sway back and forth, like heads listening to music. I need to pee but I keep it in. I don't know why and I'm ashamed about not knowing. I'm always cold. She's always cold, the mother says.

And then there's the doctor who wants to examine me between my legs. He enters my room. It's so bright outside. He approaches nimbly, calls me a name I've never heard before, meaning *champion*, a female champion, a girl champion. He says it won't hurt, what we're going to do. The mother and the father will be there to watch. A face can look like a moon. Two moons, three. I tense up. Try to look at the mother, at the father, but no one is there. Just my crotch and moons. Moons have no eyes, only flat, furrowed something or other. They want me to relax, and they try to act in a funny, light-hearted way and say crack, split, privates and their faces grow sharp as flick knives, sickles. I think about driftwood, about hard, wet, slippery pieces of plank, full of splinters. The doctor's face, as he leans close, is covered in black dots. *Girl champion.* What does that mean? What do I have to do?

Later later later. Many faces that come too close. Tongues at the periphery of my own, determined and independent. Many voices that call out to me, whisper, summon me from dim, wavering corners.

I don't know why I finally tell this to the boy, the one I wanted nothing to do with for so long. It must all sound meaningless to him. A small raccoon with a serious face. Is he right? Am I hoping to escape a world in which I've unwittingly ended up? You're a grown-up who's obsessed with the past, he says. He says it out of consideration, he wants to understand, to understand me. I remember him. He's standing in front of a painting in a big city. We're on holiday together, as a couple. We've just slept together in the heat of the room of the guesthouse where we're staying. Yes, I say. But I'm also a child who's obsessed with the future, a raccoon who will one day drop the slice of apple and make off. But how?

I want to be called mist, because the mist embraces me and makes me invisible. I suppose that's what I think a name should do. I hear my own name all the time. I'm the first child. Everybody loves the first child. No one has seen a child walk before. No one has heard a child talk before. All the words are new, fresh. Apple. Slice. The Virgin. The child. The sun is yellow like my crotch, like my name. The mist doesn't clear, and that's good.

It's winter. I've been taken to the grandmother's. The nights are bitterly cold because the house is old and dilapidated. The mother has brought a small suitcase with my things inside. Crayons, patent leather shoes, some bin liners. The father in the background, his back, lean and sinewy like a fine, narrow door. They give me thick socks to put on. Woollen underpants. Tights. Camomile tea for breakfast, camomile tea for supper. I wonder why he wants to know all this, the boy? Can't we look at the paintings instead? I ask. Yes, he says. Does he feel a sense of shame? I suppose I'm hoping he does. Why? Because *raccoon*. Because *later*. Because I'm listening with a pierced globe for an eye. And because the slice of apple isn't sad in itself, I must become a sad mist, a pierced crotch, a non-eye.

Flick knives. Moons and mist. I've asked the grandmother if I can stand in the doorway and look at the sky, because she said it might rain and that hardly ever happens. I see a boy limping down the street, walking so strangely I think he's fooling around, play-acting. As he draws closer, I see his mouth is hanging open. He's surprised, ashamed. His calf is torn up, his jeans too, as though a huge fountain pen has leaked over his leg. There's a lot of blood. I see bone, bluish-white and shrieking, drenched. The boy presses his cries back into his open mouth, almost swallowing them, looks around to see if anyone saw him. But no one is leaning out a window, no one is outside sweeping the pavement, no one is standing at a front door calling in their children. And the mad dog is nowhere to be seen either. It must have run on, disappeared down towards the river. But I see the boy. I see the bone. And then I see the dog too, down by the river. It's jaw like a sea anemone.

I look after a goat that's kept at the back of the house, by the chicken coops and a shed for tools and spades. One night I hear the grandmother talking about a child who has no shoes. Everyone is poor here, in this street. But I have shoes, nice patent leather ones, and I want to be the poor child so that they can have my shoes, and I want to be the shoes that the child can walk in, and then I can't sleep for wondering whether shoes can sleep or if I, who am both children, can sleep without shoes, if that's even possible. I hear the grandmother breathing at night. Quietly at first, then harshly. Is she able to sleep because she doesn't think about bone, sea anemones, shoes, children? Morning comes.

It begins with the door where I stand freezing, the grandmother's ramshackle place where I love to be, to sleep, to dream in when the uncles have been here for dinner and the aunts set the table and clear it afterwards, and bicker affectionately with the brothers and I learn simple yet important things. That the grandmother is also a mother and the aunts are daughters and the uncles are sons, that skin can form on milk, which I don't like, that the barrel we use to wash ourselves is dangerous to fall into for a child, that the water is sometimes cold and that puts me in mind of lead, of flick knives, because the things surrounding me are ambiguous, mysterious and mute, but not insignificant. I learn that the mother's smile isn't always reliable, that the aunt who is the mother's best friend is also a funny cousin, that one of the uncles is small in stature but enormous in other, inexplicable ways so that he becomes a pounding heart, a rumbling truck when he looks at me, lifts me up and teaches me the makes of passing cars, teaches me to cycle without stabilisers, to draw superheroes. Doesn't he know that I'm a girl?

Every day I discover new things. As if all the components of the world have been waiting patiently for me only to now reveal themselves cautiously, obligingly so as not to overwhelm me. Little by little I hear the whisperings of things. Some dust on a skirting board, a spider swaying back and forth in its web, the shape of the table leg and the uneven wear on the shoe of one of the grandmother's friends, a black-clad woman with brown tights who smells of dust and wooden floors. I find a coin. It's green, no, greenish. I am lifted onto the shop counter when the grandmother buys sugar and flour. This is what the counter looks like from up here, she says. There are the shelves of sweets. I hold out my hand with the coin in it. The man says that will get me one boiled sweet. I don't want to hand over my coin, but it's normal to hand over coins, it's the done thing. Then you're given something in return. I put the sweet in my mouth. It's called politeness. Politeness tastes bad, shameful. What do you say? You say thank you.

This is what the grandmother's house looks like. It has a bedroom facing the street. The beds are old and funny, odd, comical, I don't know which word is right. They sag in the middle like old horses, like the uncle when he lets me sit on his back and makes up horse names for himself. He's called *horse uncle* and I'm to be called *mist,* the same name as a dog in a comic strip. But I don't want to be a dog. I want to be a horse. I hope horses can be called *mist* as well. They can, the uncle says. Everyone knows that horses can be called whatever they want.

In the room next door there's a dining table, dark and heavy, impossible to lift, not even a superhero could. The uncle who's a horse lets me dance on the table, and when the other grown-ups visit I do what we've rehearsed to entertain them. They praise me. Everyone applauds. It's nice, I realise, to be looked at. No one has ever seen a child dance on a dining table, not only is it unthinkable but quite exceptional. Rarely is a child considered good enough to be allowed. But I don't like it. There's something about the silence that arises when everyone is looking at me. It's as though my chest has been left behind somewhere else, and only afterwards do I sense how uncomfortable, how strange and empty it feels. The next time they want me to perform, I say no and start to cry. *Later later later* many people will tell that story. By then I'm a big girl and have long since stopped crying. The mother says I'm a good girl, now you just need to stop shivering, it's bordering on ridiculous, all the heaters are on.

I eat fried corn kernels. I eat soil when lying on the ground. I play with two yellow fish that swim slowly back and forth in a bowl on the windowsill. I'm the child of one of the daughters. The grandmother's house is small and has a canvas roof that is always sagging and looks like a big belly, a balloon belly, like the old uncles have under their cardigans. Across the street there's a brothel and I make friends with the girls working there. I like their tousled hair, their sunglasses, and the wads of cotton wool between their toes when they paint their pretty toenails. I like the colour of the nail varnish and how they yawn and drink juice from big glasses on the pavement in the mornings in see-through dressing gowns. I'm also see-through. When I play with the fish, I swim.

The grandmother's sons all work. They drive trucks but are interested in every kind of vehicle. They'll often stand, bent over, under the bonnets of cars parked outside the house, looking like they're about to dive into the engine. They repair mopeds for the neighbourhood kids, replace gearboxes on old wrecks, lie under the cars so only the legs of their dirty, oil-stained overalls stick out. They wear steel-toe shoes that they let me stand on, then they'll dance and fool about, and spin me round like at the carnival. They often bring money and food to the grandmother, who's their mother, then leave again, to call on young women they're seeing. I can tell when that's going to happen. They drop down the bonnets, wash themselves in a barrel, and afterwards they'll smell fragrant and their hair will be smooth, black and shiny, their smiles like shrieking bones. Their hands are usually black with oil and grime and everything else the cars leave behind on them. But not when they smell fragrant. They change into different trousers than usual, lighter-coloured shirts. Their stubble isn't prickly when they hug me.

The uncles have their own places to live. Some live with a friend. Others alone. Some of them hardly live anywhere, because they drive their trucks from place to place and sleep where they eat or with their load. They'll just lie down with the furniture, the pig carcasses and the milk they transport. The uncles go back and forth between here and there, not caring much where they are, what's home and what isn't. They're as indifferent and unaffected as palindromes.

The house is full of women. The grandmother's daughters are poor, so they must live in small rooms behind dark curtains. Women's things lie here and there, scattered around the house. Scissors, combs, a globe, a warped, forgotten fiddle. The mother is the jewel of all the sisters. She has an education. She buys her coats in the finer shops in the centre of town. I am the daughter of the jewel. Jewels sparkle. They shine. I leaf through a book. I say I want a diamond for my birthday and everyone laughs, including me. Afterwards I'm ashamed, because I don't think jewels and diamonds are that nice, even though they shine. So why did I say I wanted that? If I could do things differently, I would have wished for a dog, even though I'm a little afraid of dogs. But no one here likes them. The uncles chase them off by throwing stones at them. One time the grandmother and I come across the twisted remains of a dog, a bitch, by the river, its belly torn open, and she told me that sometimes people mix broken glass into the mince so that the dogs die on their own and they don't have to stone them.

The grandmother's daughters are the mother's sisters. They're also my aunts. Many things are several things at the same time. The torn entrails of the dead dog, for example, stays with me for the rest of my life. It doesn't matter that she's dead, that she died centuries ago.

I think the aunts are grown-ups. I think everyone except me is a grown-up, but *later later later* I see their young faces, the puppy fat, the flat chests, and I hear men, more boys really, on the roof at night, like cats. They come to fetch the aunts, I hear furtive hisses while the grandmother snores. Psst. And I see the shadows of the aunts, moving slowly and carefully, further into the house. The mother says she's happy to be finished with that kind of thing and hugs the stylish father. He stands in the doorway with a bottle of cola in his hand. They have just dropped me at the grandmother's. They're about to head off. They have something important to do so I need to stay here for a few weeks. The mother's sisters watch the father as he puts on his sunglasses and adjusts his shirt collar. The mother is finished with nocturnal roof climbers. You have to set your sights higher, she says. The father takes a swig from the glass bottle. The father is also a jewel. He and the mother burn bright in the doorway like two matchsticks. Then they hop into a new, green car.

How slow childhood is. We huddle together, us women. Link ourselves to one another, sleep in old beds that sag, like the hulls of sunken ships at rest. Everything is slow and greenish, submerged. In the daytime we wash clothes in the barrel in which the horse uncle almost drowned once. My hands turn red like the aunts' hands from the harsh, cheap soap. It makes me proud to be like someone else. When the horse uncle stops by with a bag of frozen chickens, I run to meet him and ask how old he was when he fell into the barrel, if he saw yellow fish down there. Oh, yes.

Time passes, but I don't really have any idea what that means. I merely sense a movement of sorts. A piece of an earthen wall falls off and crumbles. My drawings fade if left in the sun. That the shoes, now too small for me, can be given away to someone who has the same size feet I had before, when the shoes fitted. Time is a kind of constant, a cautious shift. As though someone were carefully pushing against everything in the world with their snout. The river behind the house overflows when it rains. The street fills with water and looks like the river. I learn to fold paper boats. I help to make the food and wear a sea-blue apron that I inherit from one of the aunts. I stand on a stool next to the grandmother and watch the chickens being chopped up with a little axe. I can hardly eat a bite but can't explain why. I'm allowed to stand in the doorway and watch the falling raindrops. I talk to the sky, in my head. It replies, but what it says is so strange I don't know if it's being serious or if I'm too stupid to understand. Water, paper boats, axe, bleeding boy and chickens. Bone. Palindrome. Sea anemone and the stalk of fangs.

The weeks have passed. They come to collect me. The mother is wearing sunglasses and a beautiful coat. The father stands in the background waving to me from the new green car. I'm going home to where I actually live, so I need to give my hair a proper brush. What passes muster here is different there. It's as simple as that, the mother says. Or does she? Maybe it's something I learn myself. But how can that be?

The car smells nice. As we drive through the busy city centre streets, the father pulls over and rolls down the window to greet some friends. All I see are open mouths, the mother applying red lipstick and looking at herself in the small mirror on the sun visor while saying funny things that make the father's friends laugh. The father lights up a cigarette and the friends look at me in the backseat and ask is this the princess, as though expecting me to do something, say something, but I don't know what that might be, so I look away. The mother turns around and tells me to roll down the window. The air is cold and sharp and I have to smile and laugh at the father's friends. I'm the daughter of the jewel. Gleaming like a little soldier, I sit there shivering. Where do the similes come from? I ask myself *later later later*. Where does the soldier come from?

We drive home after that, to where I actually live. The mother opens the low iron gate. The house is newly painted. Do you like the colour? The mother asks and I nod. Childhood is slow. I have time to look at things for a long time, at how the gate opens and closes beside the mother's body. At the father, turned in his seat, as he reverses the car in the street to drive back to his friends. When I see the similarities between one thing and another, it takes on a life of its own. The soldier in the back seat is real to me, because he too is me. Strange, majestic, sad.

The mother has filled the living room with green plants in big orange pots. Climbing roses, entwined around strips of wood, now ascend towards the first floor. It's very pretty, the mother says. I stand for a while looking at it all before being told to go up to my room and wait there for a minute. The mother has a surprise for me. *Later later later* I think about the structure of experiences, the order in which things manifest themselves, about the mother's anticipation when she shows me a new blue coat, just like one of her own.

Don't drink so much water, the mother says. I take one last gulp, way too much, and spill. Spilling water on yourself is not good. I'm ashamed and try to wipe it off but my hands get wet and the water runs onto the chair, down the leg of the chair, and onto the floor, forming a little puddle below my dangling feet, and dinner is thereby ruined. But I like water. All kinds of water. The water that runs, smoothly, yet choppily in places, in the river behind the grandmother's house. The muddy, grainy water when it overflows. The water that comes in fits and starts from an old green tap. The water in the barrel we wash in, that looks like a black eye. The rain I wait for, the unfathomable sky, the clouds up there, which are only air, the mother says, nothing to worry about really. One night it thunders and I'm sure the sound is coming from the clouds. Then it rains and I get out of bed to look through the window. Here the water isn't flowing down the street. No children are folding paper boats. Nothing overflows and looks like a river. I shiver. Pee is also water. Yellowed water. There is something about what comes from between my legs when my crotch is prickly and itches, when the mother wakes up because I'm shivering in the wet bed and must tell someone. She makes grumbling sounds, her body heavy and stiff. So unlike the mother in the daytime, who is light on her feet, beautiful, radiant. At nighttime the mother needs to sleep, but I'm cold and wet so she pushes me aside with one hand, a bin liner ready in the other.

But where's the father? I think *later later later*. He comes home stifling his laughter and smelling strange in the early hours. The mother doesn't care that the racket the two of them make wakes me up. Maybe it doesn't even cross her mind. She asks about the smell but the father just sniggers and says *what smell, I can't smell anything*. I sneak to their bedroom door, peek through the gap. It feels as though I stand like that the rest of my life. That's what I tell the boy as we stand looking at the painting, in a museum, in a big city. We're almost adults so we need to share what happened in childhood. That's what he says. It's all we have. All we can offer each other.

I *offer* the mother. Hold her up for the boy, my boyfriend, as though I'd been carrying her carefully in the palm of my hand to display her, a beautiful figurine of the young mother and the scene as it plays out in a crack from the past, a door slightly ajar in the house where I actually lived as a child. I catch a glimpse of her face. A terrible face. As though it has slipped, like a skin-coloured mask that has lost its contours and caved in on itself. She grabs the alarm clock on the nightstand. It's light blue and round with two thin silver legs that make it look like a fat little boy. The father stands against a wall, grinning. He has to duck when the mother throws the alarm clock at him, and no longer sniggers or says anything as it crashes against the wall behind him, leaving a dent that never goes away.

But wasn't there a curfew? the boy asks as we stand looking at the painting. Was the father allowed to be out at night? It's an apt question. I understand it while at the same time I don't. Not yet, I say. *Not yet.*

It's cold. I shiver terribly. In a dream, I stand barefoot by the riverbank and cast a net. I catch many yellow fish. The water is feathery and soft when I sink into it, when I cross the surface like an arrow. Maybe I wet my bed because I dream about rivers, because the yellow fish find their way out through my crotch. I'm always a stranger to myself at night. I wake up, open my eyes, but distrust what I see. My dreams are deceptive, foolish. Sometimes I'm a big, white lord made of foam. Other times I'm a sort of sea goddess, because I almost always dream about water. There're no such things as sea goddesses, the mother says, annoyed, when I tell her about the dream. Everything doesn't have to be so difficult, so cold. I can understand why she's annoyed with me. She has to sleep. She needs to sleep. I've got to find something to do in my room. I imagine I'm at the house where the grandmother and aunts live and am walking to the river. I crouch down. Take out the slice of apple and wash it. I'm a racoon, a sea goddess with the face of a lord, a river girl, a water changeling, stepping out into the stream, but also into puddles, afterwards, when the rain and the flood have subsided, when the river is calm and normal once again, and the grandmother's street is full of water. Pretend river, pretend sea, goddess temple. Then it's time for dinner.

I shiver, sleep, can't sleep perhaps. The day dawns. I hear the mother on the telephone. The doctor who comes to examine me between my legs says I behave like a champion, *a girl champion.* I need to undress. I shiver. I don't kick him in the face but am then ashamed for not having done it. The doctor visits time and time again. He's nice but his face is huge, and up close to my crotch, as though he wants to sniff it. I'm afraid fish will come out of me. I tense my stomach. It's so cold without tights, without knickers on. The mother smiles. The father in the background. It's as though everyone is laughing at me, at the crack. I am a drowned flower, a sheath, a really brave girl, say the mother and father and the doctor too, but inside myself I'm all these other things.

The mother and I in blue coats in a park. The city is so nice and quiet in the winter. By the cathedral we meet some grown-ups who compliment us on our coats and I stand looking up at them. The mother tells them amusing things about me. A lot of people will eat soil, but not an entire earthen wall, she says, and they laugh. She tells them about the yellow fish I saw underwater, and they laugh some more. I laugh too, in my blue coat, or maybe it's my coat that laughs. Afterwards I'm told to go and play on my own a while. I crouch down on a patch of grass in the park and try to think of something. I look over at the mother and her friends and can tell they're still talking about me, about pee. The sun is shining. I feel like someone has lost me.

Sometimes the mother will sing to me. The song she knows, the one about the sky and the sea being almost the same. Both just as blue from a distance so it looks like they blend into one another. The mother drives the green car and I'm allowed to sit where she would otherwise, if the father was driving. She's so beautiful, I think. Her sunglasses are flecked like the fur of a tiger, shiny. They cover her eyes, a lot of her forehead and below her eyes too. *Later later later* when I start school at the nuns', one of the teachers shows us a blown-up photograph of a fly, and I think of the mother in the car wearing the sunglasses on the way to the sea and the lighthouse with me. We arrive and park by a kiosk. The mother buys me an ice cream even though I'm freezing. I understand that this is where the mother and father each come on their own when they need to think. But why bring me along?

What is a horizon? I ask. There are several words in the song that I don't understand. The mother points at a bird of prey hovering over the waves. The horizon is a border, she says. But if you look carefully, you'll discover it's hardly there. Just like in the song. See? Give me your hand.

Bird of prey. Border. Swimming isn't allowed on this side of the lighthouse. It's extremely dangerous. It's a winter day, grey, bitterly cold, the sand is damp as a bed in the darkness. The wind blows in gusts. The reeds sway back and forth, I think. I can't remember everything. On this side of the lighthouse the waves are treacherous, the mother says. Do you see? But it's as though she's looking at something other than the waves, the reeds, me. The lighthouse is so beautiful, it's the winter they paint it, repair the wall, the steps. Can we go all the way up? I ask. I'm wondering what you can see from the round tower at the top. If the waves are less treacherous. No, the mother says, maybe another time. She can't face climbing all the steps. A sign says not to write, scratch or carve on the newly painted wall. I see a heart with an arrow through. *P + EL.* The mother says she'll be right back, wait here. I sit on the wall and dangle my legs. The sand catches me when I jump. I'm a big girl now, jumping from such a height is fine. Over there the mother is walking. She's taken off her shoes and holds them in her hand. She hardly ever feels cold, or else she's making sure her nice shoes don't get dirty. Can I come with you, I call after her, but she turns away and I understand I need to stay where I am. Play by the lighthouse. I get a little scared when I see a pack of dogs, thin as partition walls, approaching. Where do the similes come from? I see the mother grow very small as she nears the water's edge. I see another woman walking along the shore, towards the mother, from the dangerous side. She's as thin as a pencil stroke, with wild black hair fluttering in the wind. They meet, in the middle of the horizon, the mother and the woman with the wild hair. The waves crash behind them, if I close one eye it looks like they'll be swallowed by the foam at any moment. Then the woman walks back the way she came, and the mother grows larger and larger as she comes towards me, her shoes dangling in her hand. I tell her about the boy who was bitten by the dog outside the grandmother's house, about the dark, ripped trousers, about the shrieking bone and his shame. The waves are huge. They rise, very slowly, then crash down and are gone. Into what? Themselves? How can that be? Many people have drowned themselves over there, the mother says, pointing. She wipes the sand from her feet, puts her shoes back on. What does it take for a verb to become reflexive, I want to ask, because I'm going to spend the rest of my life wondering about it. But I keep quiet. I don't want to bother her, and besides I'm a child. I don't know those kinds of words.

The horizon is a border. The mother paces the ground floor of the house where I actually live, smokes, turns the music up and down, then she goes to bed but soon gets up again, waters the plants at night. The father tries to sneak into the house. The sound of the key, turning slowly. The thin, creaking noise the stairs make. The gap I peek through, all this I collect without my being aware. All that is woven together, interlaced. The silences of the night, the waiting, the music up and down. The voices of the mother and father when they think I'm asleep and can't hear them.

My ears. Slow in the orange bed where I sleep, where I pee and pee, and lie and shiver and listen while staring at the emerald palms on the wallpaper, the money plants and peperomias. On the wall by the door hangs a poster of horses grazing. Trees. Bluebells. A volcano in the background, like a proud old man with his eyes closed. And the little figure of Jesus, the son of God, crucified above the desk where *later later later* I sit poring over letters, the alphabet, the slow writing and the slow reading. *Marisol.* I have the same name as the Virgin, the mother of the son of God who hangs in my room at night. And the sun, yellow, as though it pees on everything. In the daytime the doctor comes to examine me again. My crotch is a cleft, open. No one gets to sleep when I pee.

The house where I actually live. The mother's and father's house. The plants. The climbing roses. The orange bed, the volcano, the monkey bums. The mother's bed and the father's bed, big as an ocean. A small balcony facing onto the alley. The sound of a motorcycle in the early morning, when it's not yet light and the streetlights are still on. The smell of freshly baked bread from the bakery around the corner drifts through my window. The man who knocks on the door to sell milk, yoghurt and butter to the mother, speaking respectfully to her, addressing her in the formal manner, as though she were old and not him, with his ghastly hands. The father's spiral-bound calendars in the dining room, the strange dinners the mother makes. I ask if I can get fried corn, if there is any roasted corn. You're just like your grandmother, the mother says, and tells me to eat up. It's sinful not to eat up the food. The bread is the body of Jesus, she says. It's holy. On one occasion I see her about to throw a piece of bread into the rubbish bucket under the kitchen sink. What about the son of God? She gives me a resigned look, ruffles my hair and kisses the bread before dropping it among the carrot peelings and plastic wrappers. I like bread. At the grandmother's it's often stale, so we toast it and eat it with butter. There's so much more than just buttered toast. The green food is spinach. The father really likes that. Spinach and beetroot. My mouth is all red after I eat it. And liver.

That soft, horrible meat with the metal taste, or maybe it's iron, the same shiny sharpness as when you lick a climbing frame. Threatening. A painting hangs in the living room. Several mountains. Volcanoes as well. Horses and wreaths of flowers. Everything tastes of liver, tastes metallic.

People are constantly knocking on the door. Friends of the father, friends of the mother. So stylish, all of them, in their leather jackets and turned-up shirt collars and short skirts, necklaces and bracelets. They sit down on the brown sofa, the father opens a bottle and they all drink from tall glasses and eat peanuts. When there's no room left on the sofa, the last to arrive sit on the floor, on the patterned rug. The cigarette smoke, blue and languid, seems to glide wearily above the lively conversations. I'm told to stay in my room. I stare at the horses, the monkey bums, the volcano and the bluebell creepers. Come up with a game only I can play. What does the horse say to the volcano? *If you want, I can climb you.* The monkey puts on a bluebell and says it's underwear. The son of God hangs, pierced but awake, even though it's late at night and his face hangs down, bloody and exhausted. There's a smell of smoke in here. It seeps up the stairs, comes into my room, blue and shimmering, slender and weaving like a snake, like a blood vessel, like the river behind the grandmother's house in summer when everything dries up, and the river becomes as thin as a length of steel wire. I play a game only I can play. What does the Son of God say to the volcano? To the horse? *I hope no one wets the bed.*

The father has bought a silver cassette player that he brings to my room along with the hard, uncomfortable headphones I must put on. The father teaches me the right way to insert the tape and how to turn it over carefully, making sure not to break it. The songs sound strange, almost scary. The sounds get very close to my insides. Some of the songs are in another language. I really like some of the sounds. I must ask the father what kind of sounds they are, but I forget to, I think, or else he gives the same answer every time. I think it's a piano, I'm not sure. When the tape is finished, I turn it over. And when it gets to the other end I go and sit on the stairs, on the second step from the top, and peek through the climbing roses, even though I'm not allowed. I'm supposed to be in my room. Playing, making things up. In the living room, everyone is laughing but I can't make out what they're laughing about. The music is turned up and then down again. I can't make sense of any of it. Maybe that's why I remain sitting, to talk to the child I was, and ask about what, exactly?

The father looks so nice in his tan suit, a glass in his hand and a cigarette dangling by the armrest. One of the father's friends always drinks from a small glass instead of a big one. The mother and the mother's friends smoke cigarettes that are longer than the men's, except for the funny cousin who I find scary. Her laugh is deep, almost detached, as though she's always making fun of someone. A woman with freckles sees me sitting there, but looks away as soon as our eyes meet, as if she's afraid. Can you be afraid of a child? Am I a scary kid? Or does my memory fail me? Someone starts to sing, a woman the father likes very much. She sings with her eyes closed and arms outstretched, as though ready to catch a beachball or a child someone throws to her. The father is happy and light-hearted. Maybe somewhere there's a photograph from that evening. The father with that glass, that smile, as though seen through me, through my head, as though my head were mirror-like. Cigarettes protrude from the mouths. The music goes up and down, the pale, slender singer who the father likes in the sheer, white dress. He looks at her. Then looks at her again. Everyone claps her. Is he going to leave us? Would he rather live with the singer? Maybe she has a child who doesn't pee.

But the father stays. He stays and then leaves. Does both. He's happy and light-hearted. Mingles with the guests as they arrive, talking loudly and laughing, staring at the singer when she sings, then he disappears like a fishing line, and the mother and I are alone in the house for days at a time. I think about things that are many things at the same time. Volcano and father. Jewel and mother. God and son. Daughter on the stairs. Horse that talks. Bluebell underpants, the voice of the singer rising like a wave and crashing down in the father's face as he sits on the sofa with his glass.

The doctor is also down in the living room, in the deepest, most remote part of my childhood, before the country collapses. He's not a doctor at night. Then he's a friend of the mother and the father. But his head is just as big, just as close. *Something's wrong with me*, goes the chorus of a song I listen to over and over again. I like the sound of the piano, the violins and the glockenspiel and a deep sound that I think is a drum, or someone breathing out. Everything I know I've taught myself.

I want to be called *mist*. I am a sea goddess. I take care of a horse that talks to a volcano. I look at the son of God hanging from a cross, and imagine boys being bitten by sea anemones. In a picture book I'm given about Jesus the son of God, he's in the garden where they come for him on the night before he's killed. I learn about a kiss and dream of a garden, but I feel like I'm awake. And vice versa. I'm awake but see cloaked beings in the doorway. A severed ear. Scourging and pierced feet. That's why the doctor's face is also here, between my legs, along with the faces of the mother and the father and all the guests. As if nailed into me, all this. The funny cousin. The woman who looks away. The man with the ice cubes in the small glass. The singer in the sheer dress, who the father likes. They are young, but I think they're grown-ups, old, even. They are so close to my crotch, all of them, with their spectacles and cigarettes and consideration. Like balloons rubbing against one another.

And then it happens, I say to the boy as we stand in front of the painting at a museum in a big city. We've slept together in the hot guesthouse we found the night we arrived by train. I feared being robbed when we went to change money, but he held my hand tightly as he stared at a man sweating below a lightbulb. It'll all be OK, he seems to say, as we stand waiting for our money. I've told him loads. I don't know why. Maybe I want him to understand everything that is real to me. To make him aware of these things. That it feels like my life is full of mirrors, that I'm often so dizzy, and maybe that's why I sleep fitfully at night. We have slept together. Now we're standing in front of a painting in a museum. We've been talking for months. At first, I ignored him, didn't understand what he was after, why he kept calling me. I said no. I made excuses. But he wouldn't give up. He makes me happy but I'm afraid of happiness. I've never considered how closely linked happiness and fear are before. I guess I've been stupid, distracted and inattentive. Now I'm nervous and ashamed. I either speak too quickly or too slowly, say too many things at once or hardly anything at all.

And then it happens, the country collapses I say many times but don't get any further because I don't remember it happening. I only remember that other people remember it. The mother and the father *later later later* in a little apartment on the far side of the world where we must hide and live the rest of our lives like that, hidden. My happiness is a hiding place, I say to the boy as we stand in front of the painting, but I don't suppose it makes much sense to him. What about our happiness, he almost seems to say. Our happiness is when we embrace, when we make simple dinners together, go to the cinema and drink a beer at a bar afterwards, travelling in and out of each other's lives, marvelling and intrepid, like two tiny craft wandering back and forth through times and places that only exist within us. Happiness is his face in the light from a flame. A blue wallet in which he keeps a photograph of me, a song coming over the loudspeakers. *The country collapses*, I say. But then. Do I really not remember anything?

Yes, I do. Hardly anyone knocks on the door of our house any more. I never see the singer with the see-through dress again, but *later later later* I happen to hear the song she sang, that the father liked so much, and it feels like something breaks inside me. I'm so ashamed for feeling that way. So banal. I cry because I see myself, is that why?

The boy strokes my back. I'm so ugly when I cry. Oh come on, he says. When I calm down again, I try to explain to him what the lyrics of the song are about. Nothing special, an unhappy love story, commonplace. So why then has this arrow pierced me, so suddenly? Why this feeling of defencelessness. *I was there, I was there* the singer in the sheer dress sings, like the ghost she has now become.

Now the country has begun to collapse, the father is at home more. Walks round in ordinary clothes, without the stylish jacket or the sunglasses. The mother wears less makeup. Friends still come to visit but not as often as before. Still glasses, still long cigarettes, blue smoke floating through the house. I sit on the stairs. The second step from the top. I've learned to read. Which also makes me hear differently. They listen to the radio, the grown-ups, with the sound down very low. It's not only people that change. Shifts occur everywhere, if I just look and pay close enough attention. Time's ancient snout, pushing gently. Moving things, changing them. The house has become smaller, the sounds less mellow, drier almost. It's still cold but the cold is also oppressive. The curtains are drawn, even though it's the middle of the day. My birthday comes around and the mother says we ought to celebrate by having a party, and some children, friends of mine I guess, attend. There's a photograph of it. I'm wearing a light-brown dress and my hair is straight and long. This was before it went curly, before I got lice and the mother had to kill them with paraffin. I wish I could remember what I was thinking, and not only the dress and the hair.

I'm a big girl now. I'm going to start at the nuns', at the nice school the mother never attended because the grandmother couldn't afford it. I learn the word *particular,* one cold winter afternoon when the mother takes me to the nice shopping street to buy a school uniform, black patent leather shoes, tights and schoolbooks, which we then make covers for at home. But it's as if she's looking at something other than me, the books, the paper for the covers and the labels with my name. I'm called Marisol. I'll be in 1B but the mother is annoyed I wasn't put in 1A, she says so to the father at the dinner table. I know that's not my fault but I feel bad all the same.

The painting depicts a small dog. We can only see its head. I don't know what's come over me. I just want to cry today. You're a grown woman who's obsessed with the past, the boy tells me, although strictly speaking I am still just a girl. *And that's OK.* Is it? He loves me the way you love someone when you're young. In an ignorant, hopeful, curious and self-assured way. I squeeze his hand as hard as I can. What is with that little dog? Am I the dog? I don't understand.

I close my eyes. Leave the dog. Several things that do change. Fewer ice cubes in the glasses because fewer of the parents' friends sit in the living room with fewer cigarettes. The country is collapsing but I don't think I really notice. I'm looking forward to the summer, to swimming in the sea, helping the father dig a hole in the sand deep enough for the parasol to stand steady. The father takes off his shirt and looks at the lighthouse from behind sunglasses. I'm to go play by myself, see if I can find other children. I get an ice cream. Later I'm given one more, by the mother, who sits with a shawl over her shoulders because of the sun. She doesn't want to sunbathe. She gets freckles on her shoulders, which she hates. I sit in the backseat of the green car. I'm told off for not scrubbing my feet properly, now there's sand everywhere, the father says. But there's only a little, not much. I curl my toes, wish the body could suck in bad things, that pee didn't come out of it at night. Back home we eat the scrambled eggs the mother makes, absentmindedly. It tastes good, I say when she asks. Before school is due to start, I have to sit still at the hairdresser's so she can cut my hair and then, afterwards, wait while she cuts the mother's hair. They speak in low, secretive voices. The mother tells her I wet the bed, that it's tiresome for her. I leaf through a magazine with pictures of pretty singers in sheer dresses. Where is the father? I don't give it that much mind, I don't think. The mother looks so nice with short hair. It's the style now, she says in a happy voice, as we get into the car. But it's as if she's looking at someone else when she speaks. Can I cut my hair short too, I ask. Maybe when you're older, she says. We'll see.

I begin at the nuns'. The school is huge because I'm small, one of the smallest girls to walk through the sluggish doors into the dark classroom. The schoolyard is like a ship, full of girls standing in groups. We, the smallest, by some pillars, careful not to take up too much space. The older girls are as assured as singers, with their ponytails dangling and breasts underneath their school uniforms. Someday we'll be like that too, ponylike, with big voices in our chests. The silence in the classroom before a sister enters and we stand up and greet her and God and the Virgin and the son of God. I can read, almost everyone can, but those who can't are made fun of. At breaktimes they have their hair pulled, get slapped. *Later later later* I think a lot about distance. About how far apart things are, about how close a ghost has to come before it grazes you.

Ordo Fratrum. Beatissimæ Virginis. Mariæ de Monte Carmelo.

Lots of new words. Convent. Conventuals. A brown habit. Barefoot sisters in the nave of the school chapel, the cold. Places and dates to memorise. Sunday July 16, 1251. Aylesford, England. St Simon Stock. White mantles on particularly important days of observance. The Virgin appearing. All those in a state of grace will escape the fires of hell. The shepherd children of Fátima, the same age as us, imagine. Time goes slowly but also quickly. I walk to and from school with some classmates, the father doesn't have to drive me. The mother doesn't have to drive me. At the corner of the meat market there's a horrible man we must avoid so we learn to take a different route. At an intersection a few blocks from school one of us is almost run over by a bus, so afterwards we look out for one another at that crossing. After school we take a detour past the park where we can buy chips with mustard wrapped in brown paper, which all the grease turns even browner. All the things we need to think about. How grease drips onto our fingers if we're not careful. How it's possible for three poor shepherds to be found worthy by the Mother of God. What it is about the way the man stares at us that makes it horrible. How a careless bus driver can easily kill a child if the child doesn't look both ways. A cross and a string of pearls. The rosary helping us get to know the son of God and the Mother of God. The Virgin. The woman I'm named after, who told the children to return to the village and demand that the people pray. For the pope. For the conversion of sinners and of the Soviets, filthy communists.

I can picture a disgusting pair of sandals, one crooked toe overlapping another, can almost smell the odour of coffee, cigarettes and a stale mouth. I remember a hairy black mole by the nose of a very strict sister we were all afraid of, because she carried a cane that she was only too happy to use on anyone who couldn't read properly, who stammered, was nervous and shy, anyone who according to her *had no personality*. But when she spoke about the life of the prophet Elijah and the Semitic languages it was like she turned into another person, became a kind of singer too, her gaze fixed on a spot beyond us and the cold classroom, as though she were forgetting herself and remembering something at the same time.

We stand looking at the painting of the dog, the boy and I, at a museum in a big city. I was scared when we arrived here the night before, I want to say, but I felt so safe with him, I want to say. Is it because the dog is so small, is that why I can't stop crying, stop thinking about the Virgin, about the nuns, about all the Mysteries; the Joyful Mysteries, the Sorrowful Mysteries, the Mysteries of Light, the Glorious Mysteries? Would you like to sit down for a minute, he says. I look up at the dog again and feel my voice catch in my throat. I'm afraid of how it will sound if I say something. My voice is so ugly when I cry. Oh come on, he says.

The country is collapsing but it happens on the margins of life. I can see that the father moves differently, both quicker and slower simultaneously. I'm no longer a very small child. I've learned to read. I sit on the stairs but hardly anyone comes to visit. The father sits with the newspaper. I can't see his face. The neighbours fly the flag a lot. They have barbecues in the garden. Then the mother and father close the windows. I smell charred meat until late at night. I wet myself while dreaming about the crucified son. He stands outside my window. He crawls, his body broken, across the red tiles of a terrace I don't recognise. He calls out to his father, his voice stuck in his throat. My throat? His? Always the throat, I want to say to the boy who strokes my back. I pretend to be asleep, then get out of bed quietly when the mother and the father have closed their bedroom door, go down to the kitchen and fetch plastic bags, which I place on the mattress, over my underpants and between my legs. Jesus looks like an angel who has flown into the windowpane. He's so gracious, trying to bleed thin, polite trickles. What is it that creeps up my throat and lies down there so that I can no longer breathe? That's an age-old question. I'm a child obsessed with the future. I'm the one who swaps everything around. *The country collapses* and I'm going to spend my life trying to understand why my heart constantly rushes to my throat. Why my throat is the capital of my body.

The boy holds my hand. It's as though he's waiting. I glance down when he looks at me. I'm so ugly. He strokes my back. Do you want to go, he says. No, I want to stay. See a little more.

What is a marriage? It's a couple who live together, a couple who have children. There's something slow and swift about that togetherness. I'm so small here at home, my head always tilted back to look up at the mother who's in a hurry, disappearing into one room and coming out of another. She asks me, this dress, these shoes, and now and again I must help her pull off a pair of burgundy boots, which I try on in secret one day when no one is home. But I'm not able to stand on the high, thin heels and twist my ankle. Afterwards I have to hide the pain I feel when putting weight on it and I manage that. A marriage is also shouting and screaming. Doors opening or closing too hard. Conversations behind walls, muffled but fast, hurried, as though the parents' mouths were stuffed with rags. And lots of hands, fingers pointing. Go and play. Sit there. Go to your room. Don't do that, it's too loud, the mother has a headache. The father needs to read the newspaper, listen to the radio. No. Don't.

A marriage is also the child between the parents with a toffee apple, with candyfloss, with a bag of fresh doughnuts when the funfair comes to town. At the top of a rickety Ferris wheel in my blue coat. The mother tells me about Paris, about the fashion houses, Coco Chanel, an old dream, she says, looking longingly over her hometown, the lights from the city centre, the lighthouse and the sea far below. She tells me about Grace Kelly who has a headscarf just like the one the mother wears when she drives the car with the windows down in the summer. She tells me about Napoleon, about his white horse, and that he was tiny. And fat. Not the horse, the emperor! We laugh. The mother doesn't care for fat people. She herself is nice and slim. I once brought a friend home from school who the mother just refers to as Fatty. *Later later later* I forget many things. Roads, streets, squares. How the sky used to look in autumn when rain threatened. And I forget the name of my classmate. I must have called her something and it could hardly have been Fatty.

I don't like the apple I've been given. All the sugar makes me feel sick. Everyone in Paris is elegant, the mother says, as the wheel goes round once more. It's a little scary but the mother laughs and waves to the father standing below, in the background, with a cigarette in his hand. He laughs too as we pass him. A marriage is also laughing at the same things. I hold on tightly. I want to laugh as well. My mouth is sticky, full of bitter caramel. The mother says it's an old dream, to go to Paris. She tells me about Marie Antoinette, about the wealth, the riches, the palaces, and then lowering her voice, even though no one can hear us, tells me about the French Revolution, the anger of the people, beheadings.

My friends, who are they? The girl who was nearly run over by a bus. The girl who is never allowed to play after school. The girl who has a ponylike big sister with breasts and plaits. The girl with paler skin than the rest of us, with the odd-sounding surname from Germany, who all the girls like the best. The girl I play with after school, in a house much bigger than our own. The girl I borrow a tennis racket from, a wooden one. The girl who drinks a glass of something green and sour served to her by an old woman with heavy hips who doesn't look at us children. The girl who invites me up to her room to play with dolls, with a pink pram the dolls can sit in. The girl whose father is abroad so much. I've never heard of anyone who's been abroad. I don't even know what it means. Yet I picture her father, small and plump like in the photographs in the hallway. In my mind's eye he's standing by an aeroplane. I've seen pictures of people standing beside aeroplanes. He's bought dolls and toy vacuum cleaners and aprons. We can play mummies and daddies, my friend says. I'll be the mummy, she says. I don't want to play but all the same I say: I can be the baby. I can sleep in the pram. I can be wheeled around and fed and say nothing at all, just you watch.

Sometimes the friend is nice. Other times she becomes cross and makes me feel stupid and annoying, but when I say I'm going to leave she changes and becomes nice again, and then I stay after all. But what's her name, what's she called, the best friend?

I learn to wake up, to get up before the mother, remove the plastic bags and go back to bed. And then I pretend to be asleep when the mother wakes me. She pats the bed. I lower my eyes. It's dry, I know it is but I'm worried just the same. The father in the background, walking between rooms with a towel around his waist after showering. A small radio to his ear. The country has collapsed. *Later later later* I find out everything about this time, but for the moment the days are filled with ordinary things. The school route. Chips, ice cream, superheroes on TV. Long afternoons when I play alone in my room. Supergirl. Superdog.

I don't know what the boy wants to know when he asks about the country collapsing. After arriving at the guesthouse the night before, we go out to change money and eventually sit down at a pizzeria close to the train station to eat. We order red wine and that comes in a carafe and we get tipsy. I'm happy he's here with me. I'm looking forward to seeing all the things we're going to see together. Later, we sleep together and it's nice. I try to sleep but he lies reading with the bedside light on. I twist back and forth like a dress in water, like someone who drowns herself and only in death becomes free. Where do the similes come from? I turn and look at him. He doesn't take his eyes off the book. What is it? he asks. I wonder what he needs to hear. I'm ashamed to say things that make no sense, fragments, glimpses, things only I can connect, or can only be connected within me. It occurs to me he may want to hear about the politics, the struggle of the proletariat, the factories and the beauty this time is imbued with when the father tells me about it in the little flat we'll one day live in, the one by the forest *later later later*. He puts the book down. I hear the father's voice in my voice. But not the father from childhood, the father from later, the father who unwraps the newspaper from his face after we've fled over the mountains. The father who is always in the background until he isn't, until he barges in almost to the very centre of my life. The father searching desperately for a companion, a friend maybe, a drain to empty his sorrow, his sadness, shame at having to leave his country, for allowing himself to be chased off, at having to haul his cowardice with him across the mountains, all the way to the other side of the world, where happiness and everyday life is a hiding place waiting for us, pleasant and demanding.

Maybe life is a series of rooms. The house I awake in. The green car we flee in. *The hotel*, the place where *later later later* I become familiar with all the shadows. The guesthouse, yesterday. A museum, in front of a painting of a small, helpless dog. The father who goes grey talking. When he first takes notice of me, he needs me so much, I say. The mother too. Male friend and female friend, son and daughter.

How can you say everything? How much room for love is there in someone who loves you the way the young do? There's room for the happy times maybe. For what happens before the country collapses. The optimism, joy, faith in the future. The government administrating and reorganising the health care system. All the positive things taking place in the educational institutions. Streets full of nurses, truck drivers, men in rough safety shoes. Expressions of solidarity. Free milk in the schools for children from low-income households. The black and white world that belongs to the mother and father. Their recollections. And mine.

I repeat the father's many words.

Nationalise.
Key industry.
Copper mines.
Banking system.
Telephone company.
Agricultural reform.
Redistribution.
Land expropriation.

The boy is my first love. The first to see and hear. Who has room. Who wants room. Fearless, patient. He wants to know why I like certain songs so much. *You're lost, little girl*, a singer whispers the first night I sleep at his place. He comes from a normal family, he says the first time we kiss, after I've asked, sitting on a rock by a lake on a clear summer night. I've heard about you, he says the first time we meet, on a train packed with young people dressed for winter on the way to a concert at a big venue on the far side of the capital. You're the one with the fangs.

I'm reluctant to talk at first. Ashamed. There are too many loose ends, too many trivialities. One evening I talk about intangible but perceivable moments. It isn't about remembering as such, but reflecting on the sort of relationship I've had to the world I've lived in. Maybe it's just something I imagine. He says I shouldn't feel obliged to tell him if I don't want to. But what can I say that can make sense?

The mother arrives home. Opens the front door and calls my name in a strange voice meant to sound calm. I know the mother well. She's wearing a green dress, same as the last time I saw her. Her gaze is flitting, restless, as though not landing on anything at all. She helps me into my coat and takes me to the car. It's the middle of the day. The sun is shining yet it's cold. I sense something is wrong. I notice the mother is nervous, clumsy. She drives too fast, too slowly, honks the horn and shouts out the window at people crossing the street, at other motorists who blow their horn at her. The cigarettes she smokes always make me feel sick. I'm not allowed to roll down my window because of the draught. I could end up with a droopy mouth like an old aunt. For evermore. And you don't want that, do you? the mother says, stubbing out the cigarette. We park outside the cinema. She allows me to have a fizzy drink, popcorn, even an ice lolly, which soon melts, running down over my hand and onto my coat. But she doesn't notice. She sits perfectly still in the darkness. The story of Perseus and Medusa plays out on the screen. The mother and child on a raft, sent to their deaths. The gods who save them and what a beautiful man Perseus grows up to become. A bronzed chest, blue eyes and the kind of lips I am always on the lookout for *later later later*, at parties, at summer camp, or when the big brothers of friends barge into rooms. A shadow enters the movie theatre. The shadow has long, wild hair and smells of vanilla. She sits down beside the mother. Just watch, the mother says when I ask who the woman is. A shield, a cloak, winged sandals and a monster that is beheaded, finally. The blood flows into the sea, which is Poseidon, the god of the sea. Then a horse is born. From the blood of the mother and the water of the father's body. The winged horse. The woman with the wild hair stands up in the darkness and leaves the movie theatre. I want to be named Perseus too.

Later later later Medusa shows up next to the father, who sits in a kitchen on the far side of the world and has become a different person. He pours his tears over me because some fellow teachers have been found decapitated in a ditch outside the capital. *Later later later* Medusa appears in a dream dressed up as a French queen, headless, sprawled and muddy. I look at the boy. He is my first true love. I want to tell him about Pegasus, about the father's colleagues, about the ditches and the rivers where I come from, full of corpses floating like dresses. Where do the similes come from? I go back to his place. I lie to the mother and tell her I'm spending the night at a friend's house. Whose? she asks absentmindedly. I say the name. Which one is that? she asks. The skinny one, I say. Her I like, the mother says.

Now that the country is collapsing, it's quiet in the daytime. But because I can't sleep, I hear noises at night. Distant bangs, cars driving too fast, a shuffling wind, shadow beings rubbing against the walls and lampposts. I eye Jesus hanging on my wall, gangly and frightening. I try to take a good look at him, because everything about him scares me and I don't want to be afraid. His wounds. His gaze. His crown of thorns. Everything I'm afraid of makes me feel ashamed. I'm a coward. I'm ugly when I get scared and cry. I'm ugly when I pee myself too, when I can't help but leak. I'm frightened of my dreams, of everything I don't know, but also of everything I know. The father's face behind the newspaper. The radio, barely audible. The mother helping me into my coat and driving to the sea, to the lighthouse, where she tells me to play while she walks towards the waves on the far side where it's dangerous, where people drown. Then I see her stand there, like a matchstick in the wind. Alone at first. Then along comes a woman, thin as a pencil stroke. They stand there for a while, the mother with her short hair, beginning to grow out again. The other woman, her hair constantly in her face. She keeps trying to take it from her eyes, like she's playing with seaweed.

I sit on the wall. Watch the mother come back towards me. Where is the father? The pack of dogs draw closer, the mother picks up a stone she finds on the sand, and the dogs beat a retreat on their own. We drive home, the mother is calmer, asks what I'd like for Christmas. It's as though we've been waiting for a wave to break exactly where we were standing, but it hasn't. The relief of the mother. The relief of the child. I'd like roller skates. The mother gives me a sceptical look but, in a playful way, says she'll see. After we get home, the mother leans close to the father and whispers something, and then I must go to bed even though it's far too early. I've turned off the light when I hear a gentle knocking downstairs at the front door. I sneak out of the room and sit on the stairs. The doctor is here. He looks dishevelled, distressed. The following evening the funny cousin comes to the house. She also looks dishevelled, sits on the edge of a chair holding a blue bag that she clasps close to her chest. The father places a hand on her thigh. So does the mother, and gives her something to drink in a yellow plastic glass. One morning I awake to find a young man in the kitchen when I go down to put the plastic bags in the bin. He sits bare chested. He looks like Jesus, except for the short hair. I won't stay long, he says, as though I had asked. The next time I come down he's gone.

Lots of new words. Some you can say, others you can't. Curfew. Comrade. Communist. At school the sisters teach us many things that we girls need to learn. About the importance of respecting the flag, about brave, visionary leaders, about how earthquakes occur and how often. We learn words like sediment, rudimentary, loam and igneous.

The summer holidays are slow and hazy. Do the father and I dig a hole for the parasol on the beach? Do we have a visit from a second cousin who I play with? I've outgrown my school uniform, outgrown my shoes, and the mother takes me to buy new schoolbooks, which we make covers for, but it's as if she wants to slam a door the entire time we're doing it. When I go back to school I'm no longer among the smallest girls. I've grown. My hair is a little shorter. The mother has allowed me to have it cut, but in the first week the mother and the father are called in to see the headmistress. I'm to come with them. Short hair is for boys and radicals, the headmistress says without looking at any of us. The mother and father hold hands. It's the first time I've seen that. We'll overlook it this time, says the sister, standing beside the headmistress. The mother lets her hair grow out again. How stylish she looks, with her headscarf, her sunglasses, her longer hair waving in the wind like a brown, swaying sea, like a herd of galloping horses, the falling shadow of a mountain. How beautiful she is. How I love her.

The father sleeps at home at night. He doesn't go out late in the evening any more. He doesn't come back smelling strange. No slow-turning key in the keyhole any longer. A marriage is soft knocking at the door and glances exchanged across the room. People call by and leave very soon after. A small radio, turned down low. Ordinary dinners, rice, potatoes and pieces of meat I don't have to eat if I don't want to. I look at the hanging son. I have a picture book with the whole story in it. I can read. I look. What else can I do? The garden where they come for him at night, a severed ear, the nails through his feet. Things that will follow me the rest of my life, like a litter of puppies who decide it's me they belong to.

The sisters teach us about God and Jesus and the Virgin. The night is pierced by the sound of distant shots, as though someone is playing cowboys and Indians on the outskirts of the city. Only at dawn does it grow quiet. Then I hear the motorcycle of the neighbour, who's a policeman, as he drives off to work. I smell the freshly baked bread from the bakery. The plastic bag is wet but the bed is dry. The mother, tired and irritable, comes into my room, tells me to go wash, put on my uniform, and pour some coffee in my milk to wake up properly.

One night I have to go back to the grandmother's. I'm thrown into the car. I'm still in my nightdress and am driven off by either the mother or father, and one of them has packed a small bag with socks, underpants, shoes and the school uniform. We drive through streets I recognise, streets we sometimes drive through in daylight when the mother or father drive down to the lighthouse. I lean my head against the window. I'm so tired. I'm cold, especially my feet. They've forgotten to put socks on me. The lights make tracks. In me? On the car window. I still see them, whatever that means. Probably nothing. When we arrive at the grandmother's house it's still nighttime. It's the first time I see the night, not from the darkness of my bedroom, but as though I was inside it.

Lots of cars are parked outside the brothel across the street from the grandmother's house. I've never seen the sign above the front door lit up like it is now, but I recognise the sounds. People queueing, engines starting, car doors opening and closing, the loud chortling of men, and the ominous overlap of shouts, like a drunken choir singing just what they please. The music is muffled, confined and distant. I glance quickly over at the entrance as the mother and father tell me to hurry, wake up, get out the car. The light inside is orange, as though I'm looking into a maw, an open mouth on fire. A line of men stand waiting to get inside. There's a long flight of steps, I know that, because I stood there once with my aunt and looked down towards the basement, towards the *discotheque*. Some of the women are leaning against the cars. Smoking. Stop looking over there, the mother says, crossly. I think she means me, but it's the father who sighs, lifts me up and carries me to the grandmother, who stands bewildered in the doorway, embarrassed about the sorry-looking nightdress, the worn-out, uneven slippers and the threadbare shawl over her shoulders. I was asleep, she says, as she tries to fix her hair. Come in, come in. Her mouth smells stale but I'm very happy to see her.

The grandmother's house is the same, but different as well. Time has passed. Things have shifted. The aunts are older. The boys they're in love with no longer need to climb on the roof at night and sneak in through a window. Now they come to the door, freshly showered, fragrant, their hair combed, and they are polite to the grandmother, who asks what they want, even though she knows exactly what they want. The uncles have beards and boisterous friends who stand stripped to the waist, loading sacks on and off the back of the trucks while the girls from the brothel whistle at them from behind their sunglasses, their long glasses of juice, while chain smoking on the pavement. Then the uncles leave with their beards, their friends and their trucks. After a few days they return to the grandmother's house. Wash. Change. Go out the door as it starts to get dark and I must go to bed.

It's too far to walk to school from here. If the horse uncle is at home he drives me to school in the mornings, in his red truck. He doesn't play horse with me very often any longer, only on the odd occasion. He says I'm too big now and he's too small. The grandmother waits at the school gates in the afternoon when school is finished, then we board an overcrowded bus that turns this way and that, and eventually spits us out some distance from the house, like the whale spits Jonah out in the Bible, I imagine. I wash myself in a barrel, eat dinner, sit on the lopsided bed and do my homework. The grandmother asks what the book I'm reading is about. Jesus, I tell her. She blesses herself and says Jesus protects us all, fortunately. Yes, I say. The sisters at the school say the same thing. Sometimes when they talk about him, Jesus sounds like a soldier, an armoured superhero bursting with muscles and loathing for the villains. But when I think of him, he's thin, suspended. How can such a scrawny body protect anything at all?

At the weekends, when the father and mother don't come to collect me, I stand in the doorway looking over at the girls from the brothel, lounging on the beach chairs they carry out onto the pavement in the morning. They haven't forgotten me, even though it's a long time since I was here. I wave. They raise their glasses and cigarettes. Later, when the youngest aunt takes me along to buy sugar, I get to stand talking to the girls, and they ask me if I've started school, what I've learned, and if I can read. They compliment me on my clothes and ask the aunt if she'd like a cigarette. No, she says, looks at me and blushes. But one night, when I wake up and sneak over to the window to look at the orange maw, the cars and the glowing sign, I see the aunt over there, behind the tall blonde, with a cigarette in her hand too.

The father is at work. He must serve in another city. He's been sent there by his new boss. A commandant. The father works with children, teaches them to play ball, to run, to stay in shape. He comes by the grandmother's house to collect me when he can. Stylish, in his leather jacket and sunglasses. So *that's* your dad, says one of the girls from the other side of the street and ruffles my hair while she looks at the father. I stop liking her after that.

The mother is also at work. She now has to be on duty somewhere in the valley, past the dam, towards the mountains. Her new boss has decided that. A commandant. The mother works with children, teaches them poems and songs. She's tired when she comes to collect me, removes her shoes, asks the grandmother to make her a cup of tea, lies back on the sofa and criticises the paint in the living room, it's peeling off, criticises the kitchen cupboards, they're dirty, criticises the bread she's given with her tea, it's hard, stale, almost impossible to eat.

I've learned the names of the girls outside the brothel, the friends of the aunt. Such beautiful names. Jaqueline. Mirka. Stella.

The grandmother says the parents are coming to collect me, so I need to pack my bag. I wait all day but the parents don't come until the next morning. They put me in the car. That's how I recall this time. Back and forth. The mother puts me in the car. The father puts me in the car. Sometimes the mother forgets to pack socks and underpants and schoolbooks and then I must lie to the nuns at school and they look at me and don't believe me and I feel ashamed. The father smiles and asks me about school, but when I answer, when I say that the mother forgot the schoolbooks and that I'm cold, it's as though he's looking at something other than me. Sometimes both the parents come to collect me. They wear sunglasses. They're young, stylish. How I love them. I don't really want to leave the grandmother, but I have to love the mother and father more. Today we're going to eat deep-fried fish. Today we're going to visit the funny aunt. Today we're going to the cinema. Today we're going to take a little trip to the lighthouse where I have to play by myself for a while.

I jump down from the wall. The sand is warm and smooth like the mother's skin. I watch the father walk along the shore, towards that stretch of the beach where the waves are treacherous. He also knows the thin woman with the unruly hair. The mother sits in the car, smoking and watching out. I see all kinds of things when I play by myself. I may not understand everything, what it all means for example, but it cosies up to me, wants something from me.

The father listens to the radio in the car. He turns up the volume. Sometimes they play that singer he likes so much. Other times the news is on, then he turns it down. At home he has a small radio he often holds against his ear. Once, when the father doesn't come home, I find the radio. He hides it in the cubby hole where the mother stores tinned food and matches. I press on a button. Men speaking quickly through a cloud of interference, as though the voices were coming from far away. I picture astronauts, outer space, lots of black stars in a white sky. There are many words I don't understand, many things that don't make sense. Now and then the father needs to sleep after collecting me at the grandmother's, when we come home to the house where we actually live. I ask him about the mother, where she is, but he's already begun to snore. Then I walk around the house like a ghost and touch things.

Occasionally the mother also needs to sleep after she collects me. She lowers the blinds, asks me to help. It smells of dust in the house, stuffy. The mother needs to lie down for a while, she's very tired. I ask where the father is, if he's coming. But she tells me not to be stupid, how would she know where the father is?

Back and forth. New things and the same things as before. Have I said this already? I learn the names of the girls outside the brothel, the aunt's friends. Such beautiful names. I also learn the names of all the uncles' friends. And the aunts' boyfriends, who come to the door well-groomed and fragrant, and take them to the city centre to walk in the park. And everyone knows my name. Marisol. Named after the Virgin and the sun. So nice to see you again, Marisol, they say. Are you back again, Marisol? they say.

I go down to the river and play by myself. I find a stick and play with it. I find a particularly nice stone and play with it. I lean against a tree standing crooked over the water, where the river is narrow and calm. I'm friends with the stones, with the tree, with the water. Sometimes the water is clear. Other times it's murky. I find a tyre and play with it for a while. A little further up, where the river is bigger and more dangerous, people live in shacks that look like a rubbish tip from here, like someone has thrown loads of empty cans and empty bags in a pile. There are lots of thin dogs up there too, rummaging through the rubbish along with children who don't wear shoes, even in the winter. I ask the grandmother why they don't have shoes. She tells me she didn't have shoes as a child either. But now you have shoes, I say. Now I have shoes, she says and lifts her foot.

The parents collect me. There are lots of things I

want to ask about but they're tired. How come the river grows and shrinks. Why the dogs are so skinny and yet so scary. Is Jesus a skinny dog, a wounded dog, covered in gashes and therefore also dangerous? The Sisters at the school say Jesus kills Satan. That Satan is a communist and that's why Jesus kills him. I wonder if Jesus had shoes. There are many things I want to tell them about too. About the girls outside the brothel with such beautiful names. But the mother doesn't like me talking about them. Nor does the father. Jaqueline asks if I can read. Mirka says I have such nice lips, and I get embarrassed. Stella also has green eyes. I try on her sunglasses but they're far too big.

One night I stop peeing. I feel a pressure on my crotch, in a dream. I'm in a white room. In one of the corners, I see a little hatch and I understand that it's the way out of the dream. I walk over, crawl through it, and wake up abruptly. I get out of bed quickly, even though I'm cold. Open the door, hurry down the hall, switch on the light in the bathroom and pee in the toilet. A significant night. I sit on the toilet and hear the pee against the white bowl. Now I know how to get away from the dreams, away from the pressure on my crotch. I just need to find a hatch. I make up my mind never to wet myself at night again. I stare at the tiles on the bathroom floor and promise them I won't pee on myself ever again, and then I feel ashamed for talking to the floor and promise Jesus instead. Dear Jesus. I promise never to pee myself again. Afterwards, when I get back into bed, I say it many more times. Dear Jesus. Is it true that Jesus keeps us all in his thoughts? Satan, the communists and my crotch as well? Yes.

Spring is coming. I'm not quite as cold any longer. The parents are happy. The bed is dry every morning. No plastic bags in my underwear, no tiredness or frustration, because the mother can sleep all night without interruption, and then she gets out of bed and pours coffee in my milk to wake me up properly, like how the grown-ups have it. It's summer, almost the end of summer. We've been to the beach. The father held me while we swam. I don't find the waves so scary any more. I like when they come at me, foaming white, and I have to jump, and I scream, but I scream with joy. Once, a wave catches me and I roll underwater while sand swirls around me, slow and playful. I have my eyes open. Everything is moving, waving to me. A wreath of snails, algae swaying back and forth like naked trees, like drunken, happy grown-ups. Is water a kind of wind? I see the father's white feet hurry towards me. When I come back up, when he's taken hold of my torso and pulled me to the surface, I taste salt in my mouth, in my nose. I can't breathe for ages. But then I can.

The bed is dry. The country is collapsing, but I don't notice anything. It's my birthday. I get a new coat, just like the mother's. I get a new bike. I get long, white gloves. I get new, black patent-leather shoes, a pink toy vacuum cleaner, a plush nightdress, a very expensive and exclusive Italian doll that can say *mamma*.

We prepare for what lies ahead. Our first communion. The nuns teach us everything we need to learn. We are all baptised girls, free from sin. We learn the Commandments, the Creed. Some of the older girls gather us in the schoolyard and tell us secrets. It's as though we're standing on the threshold of an opening. I think about the door to the brothel over the road from the grandmother at night, glowing, pounding. I go along with the mother to look at white dresses to match the white gloves. I have to look my best in front of the priest. Some of the older girls say the wine tastes acrid. That's a word I don't know, so I have to ask the mother what it means. A lot of the other words are also unfamiliar. *Piety, chastity, libertinage.* We need to confess our sins. We hear the word *sin* all the time, but I'm not quite sure what it means either. A priest visits the school, a shapeless man in robes. The Father is important and special. He is the one we are going to confess our sins to. Some of the older girls say we should just make things up. For instance, that you stole an eraser or wanted to steal an eraser, it makes no difference. *All the sins of life*, the sisters say, they are what the Father wants us to confess. I haven't stolen an eraser. But I want to be forgiven, so I tell him I wanted to steal an eraser. The Father asks me if I touch myself between my legs. Yes, I say. I wet the bed. But not any more. He grunts. I'm granted heavenly forgiveness.

I pray to Jesus. I get beautiful mantillas that I wrap around the doll who says *mamma*. I don't wet the bed any longer because I'm a big girl. I have the forgiveness of the Holy Father and of heaven. I'm often thrown into the car, to be *dropped off*. The grandmother stands waiting at the door and many things repeat themselves. I play by the river. I sit on the uncle's back although I'm far too big. The aunts' boyfriends ask me about school, ask if I can read. One night I'm picked up again. Was anything different that night? *Later, later, later* I try to picture all of it. As though searching for a hatch in a dream. Did I overlook something? Was there any indication, back then? Should I have paid more attention? What does this shame want from me? It's hardly my fault if I didn't understand that this *pick up* was different. It's normal for me to travel back and forth between the houses. After all, I'm the kind of child who is constantly being picked up. Should I, nevertheless, have noticed *what exactly*?

We wake up to knocking at the door. The grandmother gets out of bed and shouts: who is it? The mother and father enter the dark hallway. They look unkempt. Their eyes are like saucers even though it's the middle of the night. I'm thrown into the green car. It smells of smoke. The parents say I'm going to get to see the capital. I hope I turn around and see the grandmother standing in the doorway with her tousled hair one last time. I hope I take a proper look at her house one last time, at the street, I hope I notice something in particular on the other side of the street, the brothel's vivid mouth, where all the men stand in line, the cars with engines running and the girls in fur-like clothes sashaying back and forth on high heels. I hope I noticed that something was different that night. I hope I don't just think everything is the same as always.

We drive out of the city as it's getting light. I never see the city again. Never see the grandmother again either. Not the aunts or the uncles or the friends, the ones whose names I no longer remember. Am I awake? Do I sleep in the backseat as the parents hurry out of the city? I'm standing in front of a painting, in a museum in a big city with a boy who is my boyfriend. I picture the sun slowly coming up behind a hill. I see the ocean sparkling. A small helpless dog. I am eight years old. What does that mean, that I have turned away?

I don't know how long we drive. I probably fall asleep in the backseat. When I wake up the car has stopped in a dusty parking lot. The father stands in the background talking to a man. We go into a roadside cafe. This is where the uncles usually eat when they're working, the mother says. She pushes a plate towards me. I take a bite. I don't like onions. The mother blows smoke from the corner of her mouth. The father stands in the background talking to the owner. We're going to see the capital, the mother says, keeping her eyes on the father. He's talking on the telephone, his back turned. Afterwards we get back into the car. We exit the motorway. It's a beautiful day, the sky is blue, with white stripes scrawled across it. If God is the father and Jesus is the son then maybe Jesus has been messing around and drawn squiggles on the sky because God is busy and the child must play by himself, find something to do. I'm talking too much. I'm told to be quiet, play with the doll that says *mamma*. We leave the main road and drive towards the mountains. I'm tired, made lazy by the sunlight. The mountains look like donkeys that have fallen asleep. There are almost no cars on this road, only the occasional rickety truck with leathery men in the back. We're going to visit someone, the father says. I thought we were going to the capital, I say. That's right, the father says. But first we're going to visit some friends. I fall asleep again. When I wake up the father is standing in the background talking to a woman. The mother is sitting in the car smoking, keeping an eye on things. I'm hungry again. You'll have to wait, the mother says sternly. Afterwards we need to take all our things from the green car and carry them over to a blue car. The backseat is ripped. Foam sticks out through the red leather lining. Don't pick, the mother says. Then we drive back the way we came. My doll, the son, asks no end of questions. The father and mother tell me to be quiet. They're tired, they say. I roll down the window. The air is warm. I think about the mother's hairdryer and pretend my hand is a superhero or a bird flying at speed over the mountains and the barren land. I see people bent over in the fields. They're picking something. Stop nagging, the mother replies when the son wants to know what the people are doing. On the way we must stop for a flock of sheep. The father honks the horn. The new car is old. The windows are hard to roll down. It smells strange. The floor is dirty. The horn sounds different. The sheep stand looking at us. The father swears but the sheep don't understand what he's saying. We eat at the same cafe again. I get a strange soup. I don't like onions. The father borrows the telephone. Afterwards we get into the car and the mother turns around and says we're going to the capital. I can't wait. But what about school?

The country is about to collapse but I don't know anything about that. I only learn about it *later later later* and that's how the story is full of holes, I say to the boy as we stand in front of the painting. That's how the story looks to me, like a poem by Sappho. He smiles. He likes me. Has done for a long time. And he understands what I mean about Sappho. Something perforated can also be beautiful, or at least understandable, when I talk about it in this manner.

I don't know what's the matter with me. I'm drained. Like my body is telling me to give in. As though it needs caring for. Is talking good for me? What if I don't know what I want to say? What if the boy doesn't want to hear it or if what he does hear doesn't make any sense? I could've talked about equations. I could've spoken about things that are true or untrue or both at the same time. I see the green car left behind by an adobe house. Do I wave to it? I hope so. I could've spoken about arithmetic. Two adults plus one child. One child who is a child, plus one child who will grow up. My name. The Virgin plus the sun. A green car plus a blue car. Then plus now plus later. My country minus my country.

I could have spoken about fear, about everything that happens *later later later* in the middle of the story. The presidential palace, torture, the air force, generals, all those who disappear and disappear after being shot against a wall in the hometown. But I can't face it. Instead, I tell him about living with some relatives in the capital, and in a red hotel room after that. I get to see the grand avenues. I get to visit the Palace of the Inquisition. The huge cathedral. I tell him. I say: while the family waits to escape from the country that is on the verge of collapsing, I get to sit on a stuffed horse in my blue coat. Someone takes a photograph. It's not a very good story, I can hear that myself.

First we live with a second cousin of the mother. A pale, very tall man in washed-out clothes. Over the course of the few days we stay in his spare bedroom, he constantly bangs his head against the doorframe, as though he forgot he was inside a house. I hardly sleep, neither do the mother or father, but we act like we do. I go with the mother to an office. The mother is nervous before we enter but when we go inside, and she greets the man behind the desk, she's very beautiful, very stylish. How I love her. The man is stern in the beginning but then he laughs at something the mother says and offers her a cigarette. We walk through the shopping street and the mother buys me crayons and a nice big drawing pad. The father gets up early. I see him standing in white underpants in the blue light of early morning and driving off before daybreak. The second cousin and the mother drive after him and return hours later in the second cousin's car. Did I get to say goodbye to the blue car? I hope so. That afternoon the parents take me to the city centre and we eat at a nice cafe in a pedestrianised street. I've never heard of a pedestrianised street before, only streets with cars. The woman serving us calls me princess. I say I'd like one of the cakes with sprinkles on it. Coming right up, princess, she says and looks at the father. The mother is in a bad mood but afterwards she gets to pick out a dress from a nice shop and then everyone's happy.

One day the woman with the wild hair shows up,

the one the father and mother have met at the lighthouse in the hometown. I recognise her body, the same clothes as always. But her face is much older than I had imagined. Maybe I just thought she was younger because she was thin? All the old people I know are much fatter than her. The grandmother, the sisters at the convent school. The woman with the wild hair greets me politely and doesn't look at me again. But I look at her. She hands the father an envelope. She gives the mother a quick hug, then we move into the hotel with the red room.

It's autumn. The capital is cold, grey as milk that's been left out. I huff and puff to keep up with the parents who hurry across the grey streets. I eat the grey food they buy for me. I see grey buses packed with women. Grey exhaust fumes. My lips grey with cold in a mirror. The broad, milky avenues. An unfamiliar similarity in sounds. A line of statues under the trees, founding fathers in ridiculous trousers. That's how they used to dress, the mother says and laughs. It was the fashion, just imagine. She dresses me in beautiful clothes. As beautiful as the clothes she wears herself. She's so stylish. I'm eight years old. I'm a girl. I'm the child, the mother's and father's child. I have a blue coat and beautiful black patent-leather shoes with straps. The Italian doll is always with me. Your child, the mother says. Your son. Imagine that. You're also a mother. The Virgin plus the son. What's your son's name?

I get to know the capital. It's so big. The street vendors caramelise nuts in smoking half-barrels of aluminium. We walk past the agricultural college, through a passage full of clothes shops. In my head, the river divides the city in two. It's brown, fast-flowing, full of rubbish. We're not going there, the father says.

In the morning, we leave the hotel and eat fried eggs at a cafe around the corner, not far from the railway station. Afterwards we walk under the oak trees, along the road leading to the Palace of the Inquisition, the big cathedral. I ask why it's called a palace and the mother says it's because Jesus lives there. But what does inquisition mean? The mother faces the sun. The father stands in the background. It's cold but the sun is shining. Sometimes the buildings are so high that the sky looks like the patches the grandmother sews over the holes in the uncles' trousers. Occasionally there are helicopters. I hear them before I see them. I've never seen a helicopter before, but I soon get used to them. They look like dragonflies. On the lawn in front of the Palace of the Inquisition there are lots of other families that have come to the capital to show the children the place where Jesus lives. The country is collapsing but everything is pretty much as usual. A child sits on a stuffed horse and has a photograph taken with the parents standing either side of the saddle. The mother is facing the palace. The father in the background. I'm named after the sun. I have my son in my arms. So placid, the horse, with its dead hooves on the tiles outside the church. Baroque patterns, squares within squares, triangles and rectangles. I'm eight years old. I see God's eye in the faded tiles. God's eye in the sinuous pattern of the marble steps. God's eye in the dead eye of the horse, the peace of the dead in the sunlight. The square outside the cathedral is full of families like ours. Children like me. Eight years old, with plaits and patent shoes and Italian dolls in their arms. The grown-ups buy balloons and candyfloss and ice cream for all the daughters who no longer wet the bed.

I make up my mind. We leave the hotel in the morning. Eat bread and fried eggs at a cafe around the corner, by the railway station, below the oak trees on the road that leads to the big cathedral. It's called a palace because Jesus lives there. But what does inquisition mean?

God is a dead horse. So calm. The mother holds my hand but it's as though she's holding on to something other than me. The father in the background. They barely spoke during breakfast, just stared vacantly out at the trees, the cars, and the people hurrying to a bus or to the door of a building. Something has happened. The father sat with the radio to his ear all night. The hotel room is small. I don't sleep but pretend I do. It's the first time I see fear, I think. The first time I see horror, I think. The first time I hear the word *inevitable*, I think. I hold my son in my arms. Something has happened. At night, on the radio, I hear words like *torture* and *informers*. I open my eyes. The father in the background, with the radio pressed to his ear. The mother lying with a sleep mask. She can't take the light, gets such a headache, really terrible. The woman with the wild hair comes in the morning, into our room. She's never done that before. She has lots of envelopes with her. She greets me politely and then doesn't look at me again. But I look at her.

They have murdered a poet. They captured and

killed him. He had written that the vault of heaven celebrated in the national anthem was now filled with the murderous whir of army helicopters. It's a quiet morning. Beaches and the desert recur throughout his poems. Falling bodies. The Pacific Ocean. The seabed and the mountains and snow that falls. The sky recurs in poem after poem. Sometimes the sky is a helicopter where the soldiers cut open the people's stomachs and throw them in the sea. Sometimes the sea is a sky in which the dead swim towards the mass graves in the desert. Sometimes the desert is a mass grave or a coffin and the falling bodies are snowflakes fluttering down from the mountains. The fish are the silvery coffins of the sky and the desert is a falling body through the ages. They've murdered the poet, the father says finally, even though I'm there. He has tears in his eyes. The mother doesn't touch her fried egg, isn't able to eat. They've murdered the poet. It's the first time I see grief, I think. The first time I understand a poem.

I think about what exists. The hotel room, a red carpet, fried eggs on the plates, the red rims around the father's eyes. But I also think about what doesn't exist. The boy strokes my back with his nice, warm hand and says: what is it you can't say to me? I can say everything, I think to myself. But there are still many things that don't exist, not even for me. How can I say something about them? I don't know why I think that way. The woman with the wild hair. Did she exist? Did she give me the sheet with the poem? Did she read it out for me? Or did she read it out for the grown-ups, for the father, the mother, and the other people sitting in a smoky living room a few days later, where we arrived one afternoon after taking a grey bus across the bridge over the river that divides the capital in two, brown, fast-flowing and filled with rubbish, the same river in which they had found the dead poet drowned, full of holes and slumped against an old stove someone had dumped on the bank?

I make up my mind. We leave the hotel every morning. Eat fried eggs at a cafe around the corner, by the railway station, beneath the oak trees leading to the Palace of the Inquisition. Jesus lives there. He is the son. I picture the poet hanging on a cross by an old stove. Brown, murky water leaking from his perforated body. I can't find the hatch to escape from the dreams I have about the poet, but instead of being afraid I see how everything merges: the poet, the son who can say *mamma*, the thin boy hanging with his shrieking bones, the carpenter's son born the child of the king. My dreams are filled with delicious fragrances and gifts, splendid robes. The son of God the Father has come to offer salvation. But what does salvation mean? A window? A shaft? The child lies in the manger. Still, I am afraid. I search for a hatch but find none. The child stands up and says: I will be the last thing you see. Remember me if you can, if you want, if you must. Soon the fury will come, the son says. He stands in a garden, surrounded by men in uniform, in silver-scaled cloaks of sand. Men with no gifts, with no fragrances. Fury hangs everywhere. Over the desert, over the villages, over the city streets. An old debt must be paid, says the child in the manger with his twisted jaw. I search for a hatch. The child is the debt, says the son, but the child is also the payment. The future closes like a claw around the child, around the fury, around the silver-shelled chainmail and the arm that maims the son with a whip. I search for a hatch. A tribute of sorts to the future, this killing, a soldier says. A reckoning of sorts with the past, this killing, says another. A confession of sorts, this killing, a third says. A star appears. A shrine is opened. The dreams portend. Promises must be kept. But what is a promise? A window? A distraction?

What does inquisition mean? The parents have their backs to me. They're going to show me the palace. Today we're going inside, the mother says. How beautiful she is, how stylish, how I love her, but I'm ashamed. I'm only eight years old, with my *too much*. I shouldn't be ashamed. I shouldn't have heard or seen *too much*, but I can't help it. I just see things. What else can I do? Some people just see things, that's all I can say. Or am I the one saying that?

I can't help it. I see cranes in the gaze of the stuffed horse. The movement of its flaking head. The moth in its eye. God, you old animal. With your shoulder blades dislocated at the palace. With your injured flank. With your emaciated body tossed like a garment by the riverbank. The mother wants a photograph taken of me sitting on the horse. It'll be nice. The dead horse carries me. Do I think of the horse uncle? I hope so. The father lifts me up and tells me to sit properly, sit side-saddle. I have the son in my arms. Someone takes a picture. We wait for a few minutes and then get to see the photograph. So little time has passed. *Later later later* a long time passes. Maybe I'm thinking of things like that when I think of things that don't exist. The small shiny square at first, and then us. *Later later later* we take the picture with us everywhere, in a photo album the father and mother bring with them. *Later later later* the fading, the father's trousers, that first become light blue and then whiter and whiter and the mother's coat fades and mine too, and the faces and the eyes will disappear into the square again, on their way back in time, towards that morning on the dead horse where I sit properly, sit side-saddle, before I disappear.

Someone lifts me down from the horse's back. The father in the background. Is this our last day in the capital? In the country? Do I know that? Do I notice anything is different? I hope so. I follow the mother because she wants to go into the palace and have her picture taken. The woman with the wild hair may be with us. Perhaps she's the one with the camera, the one taking the pictures. I have a blue coat, clips in my hair. I'm the prettiest girl he's seen all day, the man at the entrance says as I hand him a ticket to the palace where Jesus lives.

The mother poses by the gilded vases, by the shiny chasuble in the glass display case, by the cope. The mother by the sacristy. The mother by the chancel. By the bones of a saint who was impaled. The mother is a diamond and I'm the shining daughter. I see her stand and pose, hazy as a mirage, as though she had drifted or blown away. I need to be careful what I look at. That's a responsibility. I've got candyfloss. That's a responsibility. I've got a blue coat. That's a responsibility. I'm the prettiest girl he's seen all day, the ticket inspector says. That's a responsibility. I smell good. It's autumn. I've seen a leaf fall from a tree for the first time. It's unforgettable. I want to tell the mother that the leaf fell like a tongue licking a scoop of ice cream. *Later later later* I learn about parallelisms, about similes, about the wonder that arises when you compare one thing to another. *Later later later* I remember this leaf falling, and myself, with the coat, the hairclips and the son in my arms. I make up my mind. When I look at something I'm also looking at something else. It's a necessity. I see Jesus, hanging. He's peed himself. Pee seeps from his hands and feet. There's something wet by his ribs. I'm eight years old. I stand looking at the dislocated shoulder blades, at the dead eyes, at a leaf that has fallen, at where God is. Yes, where is God? I want to say that the leaf falls like a grown woman, like a mother who's exhausted, but pretends not to be.

I sense time. I feel it in my body. Viscous, fleeting,

almost indiscernible before disappearing, like a cartoon character who runs and runs. That day. The wet wound next to the mother posing for the woman with the wild hair. That day. My hand stroking the doll son so he won't be alarmed by the blood, the crown of thorns and the scourging. But also another form of time. I've learned lots from the nuns. That time is also measured in glass display cases, in gilded jars, in woodwork, and miracles. A ship dangles over the mother's head while time gobbles up heretics, lights fires and *consumes* them. A beautiful word. So final. *Inquisition* has something to do with questions. With witnesses. At the nuns' I've learned about the time of the Crusades, the time of the Reconquista. About the time of the Mendicant friars, the Poor Clares, and the Carmelites. About the eternal city, God's glory and the Virgin appearing to children, because she wants the children to tell everyone they should join the fight against communism. Jesus wants that too. And God. I look over at the mother. She's so pretty when she's getting her picture taken. How I love her. Do I think about the grandmother? About the classmates? I walk back and forth between the pews, the patent shoes making a grown-up click-clack sound, the son in my arms, between the miracles, the suffering and the judgement day. I tell the son the story. I'm eight years old with the future in tow. *Later later later* all the words of the future. Theomorphism, theophany, incarnation, psyche, apocryphal. I explain what I can to the Italian doll, my child, *ciccio bello*. The mother poses, lifts her foot a little like the models do in magazines. She looks up at the vault of the church, says *grandios*. The mother by the crib, by the heart of the drama, by the donkey the son will ride upon. She looks at the chalice, makes the sign of the cross and says *worthy is that which holds the blood of the Lord, gilded within.* I've learned the word *worthy* at the nuns'. It means to deserve something or that someone likes you. The mother of the crypt, of the Virgin Mother made of cork from the Holy Land. The mother of the purity, of the inviolable, irreducible and everlasting love. I am no one's mother yet. I know it's only a doll. Only a game. No angels above the mother of the child. No messenger from He who is called God the Father. No blue angel above the mother of the child's dreams. Only a pierced son with hands of piss.

It's only a doll. An expensive Italian present from when I stopped wetting myself. My child can say *mamma*. He can cry and call for *mamma*. He can move his arms towards *mamma*. But he also has gashes on his ribs, blood on his forehead, a God the Father and a carpenter father. My doll son is also terribly afraid of what the future holds, terrified of being hung on a cross, of no one watching over him until he awakes once again in his father's kingdom. That's how I learn, by dreaming, terrified in my dreams while I search for a hatch. And everything merges. I learn that the son turns into a tree, a radiant mangled branch, a little dove in the bottom corner of a drawing where God the Father is bright and shiny as a teary eye. That's how I learn that the son is also an eye, that he nods off at the edge of the desert, that time gobbles up sand. That son plus eye plus edge of the desert is one thing but also three things. That God the Father stares at the fallibilities of man for century after century. Then he sends his son down to Earth and makes him a carpenter, a cross maker.

There are many things I want to ask about. Where's

God the Father when they kill his son? What does it mean that God the Father chastises but also rewards the descendants of the dust? Is the son a demigod, son of a whole god? Or is he God the Father in the form of the son of God? How can it be that the son is also the word made flesh? And a sin offering? Transformed, changed? A changeling who speaks through his belly?

There is no one near me. The mother is having her picture taken. The father in the background. I hold the mutilated son in my arms. No one shepherds white stars. The son is killed by many, consumed. Time gobbles up everything that has begun to belong to me, eight years old, the mother and the father and the impossible child. Time wolfs down everything. I want to learn about the old gods. *Later later later* I realise it's not only child gods who are devoured. There are also people who are consumed or people who must leave where they live so that they will not be consumed. *Later later later* I think *leaving* is a way of being consumed, that *seeing* is a way of consuming yourself. I think about poets floating mutilated in the river. Once you're dead, you can no longer be afraid, can you?

The country collapses like the riverbank collapses when it rains too much. The mother is young. The father is young. I see that *later later later.* In the pictures. Their youth, fear and powerlessness like arrows loosed against a wall. And the wall is made of mist. In other words, the wall is made of *me,* because I'm the daughter of the mist. I look at the boy as we stand in front of the painting. Does that make sense?

Later later later I picture these days in the capital. And I think I can glimpse terrible things everywhere, things hidden at the time, invisible, as though childhood was a chamber of horrors I wandered through, innocent and unaware, in my coat and patent shoes, the prettiest girl of the day. I see investigators in aviator sunglasses and leather jackets. Executions carried out on concrete floors. Military doctors in soiled lab coats and cushioned shoes. Stolen infants babbling. A military academy at night and the sound of the intelligence service's car doors slamming shut. The river we cross is full of bodies. Headless, contorted men and women floating like driftwood. We're not going there, the mother says.

By the hotel there's a playground. I have to play a little by myself while the parents sit on a bench waiting. The woman with the wild hair sits down on a bench nearby. Then she gets up and walks away. Helicopters are flying in the sky. One of them flies all the way from the capital to the hometown we've left behind. It lands at the army barracks around 11 a.m. A car parks outside the gates of the prison at 1 p.m. and just before 2 p.m. fifteen prisoners are driven to the barracks. At 4 p.m. all fifteen are put against a wall and shot. At 7 p.m. the local newspaper receives a call from a lieutenant. The fifteen people executed have been condemned to death by a military court and found guilty of terrorist activity. Documents, explosives and significant quantities of firearms have also been recovered from their homes.

The father with the small radio to his ear all day long. The mother who goes out to buy some clothes. Feels better when she puts on makeup and takes a walk on her own in the city centre streets. How beautiful the mother is. How much I love her. The woman with the wild hair sometimes picks me up at the hotel and takes me to a house where I must play with a girl my own age. I don't know what we do. What the games involve. Whether she makes them up or I do. It's like I know I can't take in too much about her, the house, the afternoons, life's abundant details. It's like I already know something about disappearance, about how such imprints *behave*, like the photograph someone takes of me sitting atop the stuffed horse, the shiny square that *later later later* will besiege what is now clear, alive; sitting side-saddle on a stuffed horse, not yet indistinct, faded.

I think about responsibility. About fate. About those who are lucky and those who are not. Soon we'll leave here. *Later later later* I think about all those they came for. I think about the maws, the teeth that tear sons to pieces. I think about the word *hollow*. Hollow son, hollow sorrow, hollow country, hollow childhood. I think about left-wing students in knitted vests against a wall. Young people who wake up maimed in their hollow memories. Death is as unreasonable as a foreign language in this country from which I'll soon disappear, like a flick knife disappears, like lengths of rope disappear, like a hammer goes missing, an eraser that rubs away.

Instability. The movements that have marked my life. The car back and forth. The different beds. Staring at different objects. The grandmother with the fried corn in her apron, the funny stories she tells me to get me to sleep, but which make me laugh and wake me up instead. Then she tells me other, sadder things and I can't sleep because they upset me. And then, one day, *gone*. What? All of it? Yes, almost. Almost all of it. Sometimes, when I think this way – naked, as naked as I can – the sadness that comes over me is close to unbearable. And I feel ashamed. Of my sentimentality. Of my self-pity. Of my ingratitude.

The boy by the painting. The first time I see him I realise he is also looking at me for the first time. It's what we first have in common, this look. And that is no small thing. I've heard about you, he says, on a train full of young people wrapped up warmly on their way to a large hall on the other side of the capital to see a concert. You're the one with the fangs. Then he starts calling. When we're at the same parties, he looks at me as though through a tear, until he's had enough to drink, comes over and sits down next to me or one of my girlfriends. I'm polite, I suppose. I go outside to sit on a step and light a cigarette. He doesn't follow me, but a couple of days later he calls me up again. I try to explain that I'm not interested. We meet a few months later, by chance, in a bar. I'm waiting to order a beer. He looks at me as if I've just said something funny. He asks me all sorts of questions. I don't feel comfortable, say I'd rather hear about you. He comes from a very ordinary family, he says, the first time we kiss, sitting on a bench by a lake one clear autumn night.

And then we sleep together for the first time. The smell that fills the world just as autumn turns into winter will always remind me of him, of the flat where he used to live, cold and damp, with two broken windows that he covered with black bin liners. I inhale the smell of late autumn. Exhale with frosty breath when November comes. His father drops in occasionally with a bag of groceries. Soup, tins of tuna. His mother is very nice, very kind. He also has a little sister who is much younger. They all ask where I'm from. And I answer. The same sentences about the mother and the father and the child and the escape. *And then we ended up here.* That's how the story ends, and I see the relief in everyone's eyes when *we* end up *here*. Everyone assumes I like it here.

He's the first one who wants to know more, my first love. On the nights that we don't sleep. When it gets bright so early that our night hasn't even started. And I answer. The same sentences about the mother and the father and the child and the escape. And then we ended up here. But he remains sitting upright, looking at me. The next day I shy away. I don't know what to say. A couple of nights later he asks me again and I answer. The same sentences about the mother and the father and the escape. And the child, you forgot the child. The next day I shy away. Did I forget the child? How can that be? That day I eat with friends, drink beer with friends, dance with friends late into the night before calling at his place. He sits on the bed, waiting. My first love. Brave, curious. I'm cautious, ashamed and afraid. He holds my hand. If he could perceive a hint of the cold winter air I felt as a child – when I describe the buses in the capital, the big, silver-grey whales roaring through the streets – could he also understand the fear? Where do the similes, where does this double life, come from?

The grey cold of the capital. Lots of different cars, lots of backseats, basement rooms, backrooms. Clothes, shoes and bags. Friends of the parents. Friends of friends. All with heavy eyelids. They're usually kind to me, attentive, but it's as though they're looking at something else when they speak to me. I often sleep in my clothes, the blue coat over me. I often have to play with the children of the people we're visiting. It's not always easy. Some children are abrupt, sharp, angular, as it were. I never know what they might do. Others are so shy that they hardly dare to look at me. I sense change in the air. Time passes, days and nights. There's sun, there's rain, there's drizzle, it's so cold, it's so warm, suddenly. The mother cuts her hair and the father grows a beard. In all the houses there are small radios the grown-ups gather round. I'm told to play by myself. But I watch. I have ears big as seashells. The grown-ups turn off the radios. They fetch a guitar, some ashtrays and bottles of wine, draw the curtains and start to sing. I can't sleep. I learn the words and the melodies they play until the power goes out again and a deep, piercing silence descends. Early in the morning we're picked up by the woman with the wild hair. Her windscreen is steamed up. We can see our breath it's so cold, even though we're inside the car and the windows are closed. We cross the city, cross the bridge over the murky water. I don't want to look but I can't help myself. Am I looking for the dead poet? Am I looking for those who were shot against a wall in our hometown? Packs of dogs dig in the rubbish heaps. The buses spew out grey exhaust fumes. I think it smells good, the fumes, the petrol, it reminds me of the sputter and cough of the horse uncle's truck. I'm lying on a sofa in an unfamiliar house and have to sleep, but I can't sleep. There are too many sounds. People come in the kitchen door late at night and leave through the same door early the next morning. People have parcels with them that the father looks after, parcels that are placed in a cupboard until someone else comes to pick them up a few days later. Then I see the woman with the wild hair climb over a hedge in the garden and we must move on to other friends of hers. And every time we leave, I see less and less of the capital. Because each time her friends' houses are closer and closer to the mountains. Certain things stick in my mind. A house with a tin roof. A young woman with trainers made into makeshift sandals, the stink of her feet, and the shame on her face when the mother holds her nose and asks where the awful smell is coming from. An old man in a knitted vest standing on a chair, a big stone in his hands, waiting for a rat to emerge from under a kitchen cabinet. A huge pale woman called Kira, and a young priest, who sometimes sleeps with her, who I find very handsome and who *later later later* disappears and, years later, is found by chance in a mass grave in a desert in the north of the country. How does that song go again?

Time and time again they killed me. Time and time again I died, yet here I am, resurrected. I thank ill luck. I thank the hand that held the dagger for killing me so badly.

These are the last images I remember of my country.

Sometimes I go through them, naming them in my mind, repeating and counting them off as in a rosary. I'm afraid of forgetting. Or perhaps I'm afraid of moving on, of leaving behind. When do you do something for the last time? When do you see something for the last time? My country. I remember light-brown pyjamas, the father bribing four policemen at a mountain pass, them stamping their feet in the snow, eager to get their hands on the money so they could return to the guardhouse where a small TV screen flickered. I'm shivering with the cold. And now I see that the mother and father are too.

2

We end up in a big city, the capital of the neighbouring country, much bigger than the capital at home. The mother and father still have a little money. We stay at a guesthouse. Share a small room. We eat at a cafe just around the corner. I hold the son in my arms. I still have some crayons, stubs really, and the drawing pad. The father has a full beard, always in the background, talking to someone, borrowing a phone. How pretty the mother is, wearing makeup. How I love her. Here too we walk down a pedestrianised street. Much bigger than the one at home. I look up at the parents but it's as if they're looking at something other than me. One day they stop eating, only drink coffee, say they aren't really hungry. But when I get my food, I realise the money has run out. A couple of days later the father and I go through a metal door and down some stairs and sell a gold pendant with an image of the Virgin. That day we eat schnitzel and mashed potato. And we have fizzy drinks. We go to the cinema and watch a sad film about a creature from another planet, but when the creature can't return home the mother says she can't handle any more and we have to get up and leave. The father thinks it's stupid to pay for cinema tickets and not watch the film to the end, so we sneak into another screen where they're showing a film about a man who boxes. That was a great movie, the mother says afterwards, when the hero has beaten his mean adversary. I wonder if it's possible to be a girl and a boxer at the same time. We eat sausages with mash. Schnitzels with mash. Chicken and rice. But then the parents only want coffee again, they're not particularly hungry. One day the father and I go through the metal door and down the stairs again. This time we bring the mother's pearl earrings in a small pouch. The man on the other side of the hatch has the longest eyelashes I've ever seen, much longer than the mother's. Let's see, he says, and studies the earrings for a long time, turning them round, then puts on a pair of glasses and names an amount. The father becomes angry but he could have saved himself the trouble. The man behind the counter grins and names an even lower amount, after which the father has no choice but to nod meekly. We make our way down the stairs on many occasions after that. With a necklace, with a bracelet, with some very stylish boots and with the wedding rings.

Do I see the father is changing? I hope so. One day he looks at me and tells me he's afraid. *Afraid for mummy,* he says. But I understand that he's talking about all of us. The last time we go down the stairs to the man behind the counter, he removes his watch and asks if his belt might be of interest too. The woman who runs the guesthouse we're staying in finally gets the money she asked for, but we have to pack up and leave all the same. It's the first time I see the mother collapse. She's sitting on the edge of the bed and as she stands up her body gives way, as if her legs were made of spaghetti, as if she's fooling around. The father, in the background, is allowed to borrow the telephone. *Mummy,* I say, and she takes my hand, squeezes it and says leave me be.

It's winter. This capital city is also cold. The first night we sleep on some iron chairs bolted to the ground at the railway station. The second night a security guard takes pity on us and lets us sit in his cabin, until his boss shows up at dawn and chases us off. On the third night the mother asks if we can use the toilet at one of the large cinemas downtown. The cinema is on a wide, glittering boulevard with big lit-up signs. It's late in the evening. The last film has long since begun. We sit quietly in the ladies. After a while the lights go out and we stay there all night. The fourth night we try the same tactic again but are caught by a security guard and thrown out. On the street a man tries to rob us but the mother screams so much he gets scared, calls her a crazy bitch and slopes off. The fifth night we sleep against a wall behind some containers in a backstreet, and when we wake up the mother's handbag is gone. And so is the son, the expensive Italian doll that can say *mamma*. I start to cry. I should have been more careful. It was my job to look after the son but I fell asleep. Just like Peter, the apostle.

A few days later the father tells me to walk towards a large iron gate on my own and press the buzzer. A voice answers and I say what I've been told to say. Are you alone? Yes, I say. When the gate opens, the mother and father come out from behind some bushes in the park and run towards it and that's how we manage to get inside the embassy. It's chaos at first. You can't be in here, says the guard who opened the gate. The mother breaks down, the father puts his arms around her. Then an elegant woman comes out and asks us to enter the large house because people have begun to gather on the pavement, outside the gate, and that's not good. I'm wearing the blue coat. The patent shoes.

They make a clacking sound as we walk towards the large sitting room where we're to wait. A young woman places a plate of fruit in front of us and we eat up everything on it. Bananas, apples, grapes. Another woman enters and says hello to all of us. She talks a bit strangely and asks if we'd like something to drink. Coffee, tea. Some milk for the little one. I wonder where the son is. Try to picture him. For a second, I picture him sitting in a chair looking around for me. I know it's stupid and that I shouldn't but I begin to cry. Then the mother and father have to go into another room to talk to someone and I'm left sitting on my own. A visibly nervous man comes in with a tray of biscuits and more fruit and some sandwiches that we can eat afterwards, when your parents are finished, he says. He also speaks strangely. When the parents come back out, they're holding hands. I learn that a room on the first floor of the building is being prepared for us, where we can stay while the staff figure out how to help us. The afternoon passes. As does the evening. The mother breaks down. The father, in the background, asks to borrow the telephone but that's not possible and he remains standing with his back turned. Someone comes in and asks if we're hungry and we answer yes. The food they serve tastes strange. For dessert we're given more fruit. I eat one apple and hide the other one, in case. The following day we're driven out of the embassy in a big, black car by a man in a hat. We're told that a room has been prepared for us somewhere else in the city. That we're now someone else's responsibility.

We are to wait. Along with many others who are waiting. We're crammed together in a small room, at a squalid, cockroach-infested place that is called a hotel, but is really just a place with lots of small rooms, which the owner rents out at exorbitant prices, because the people helping refugees like us need somewhere to put the refugees, and they pay more for it than you would think.

We are to wait. Along with all the others who are waiting. Once a week the father must go to an office to stand in line. When he's waited long enough, he returns to us with some coupons, which at certain selected locations can be exchanged for bread and rice and potatoes. Once a week the father must go to a different office and stand in line and wait. When he's waited long enough, he comes back to us with some coupons, which at certain selected locations can be exchanged for a little meat. Once a week the father must go to yet another office where he must stand in line and wait. When he's waited long enough, he returns to us with some coupons, which at certain selected locations can be exchanged for milk and sugar and a little oil. Once a month the father must go to a very important office and stand in line and wait. He must wait a very long time at that place, often the entire day. One time the mother is sick. She can't take any more, she says, just wants to sleep, so I must go with the father and stand in line with him. First we wait outside on the street. The pavement is full of men who smoke and have heavy eyelids, just like the father. Many of them talk together but, every time a car passes, they act as if they don't. Many of them say hello to me, but in a weary way, as though they were about to fall asleep. When we've waited on the street long enough, we're waved inside where we wait in a hall with lots of people and lots of hard chairs. We're given a ticket and strict instructions not to lose it. On the wall hangs an electronic board with red numbers that change and we must keep a close eye on it. Our number is a long way off, several hundred away. I fall asleep, I think, but wake up because I need to cough. The father is talking to a man. The man says hello to me, but it's as if he's looking at something else as he smiles and shakes my hand. When our number finally appears on the sign, I'm so hungry I feel nauseous. We're asked to walk down a dark, narrow corridor. We knock on a door. Inside, a woman sits with stacks of paper all about her. She says the father's name, greets me pleasantly and asks if I'm all right. I nod. There's an apple on her desk, just like some of the nuns had when one of us brought one and placed it on the desk after wiping it on our school uniform. I think about all the times I could have eaten but did not. I regret that but realise it's a silly thought, a pointless thought. The woman asks the father to sit. She looks through a large file. Unfortunately, she says softly, but don't discount the possibility of there being good news before too long. You're a family after all. Many countries prefer to accept families than, for example, single men. Being a single man is the toughest, she says. Many are here for years. You have a chance, at least. Don't give up. Otherwise, everything OK where you're living now?

I stand in line. I'm hungry. It's my birthday.

And I learn about death.

Everything is dangerous. My body knows that before I do. I feel it in my legs, in the heaviness in my chest, where a sort of claw has taken hold. What can I say about that? Every time I think about the fear I picture the hotel, the walls, the tiles on the floor, the staircase and the roof terrace where the women hang the clothes to dry. I could talk about arithmetic, accumulation. Staircase plus shadows plus endless days, because I don't go to school any more, I'm just here. The only child here, at this hotel, where we wait. The mother lies in bed. Sometimes she goes down to the communal kitchen and comes back up with soup in a tin cup for me to drink. Water and cabbage, for the most part. Maybe some bread with margarine. The father waits, stands in line, comes home with those heavy eyelids. They exchange many looks, the parents, without saying anything, and I learn the meaning of these looks. No bread. No butter. No cabbage. We must wait. Let the child go and play by herself.

One day the father travels up to the delta north of the capital to help somebody with something, and he returns with foreign money in his pocket. He tells me the names of the presidents on the banknotes. I walk downtown with him, forty blocks along a boulevard full of cars and buses honking their horns, and we turn onto a side street close to the guesthouse where we stayed before, through a metal door, down a flight of stairs. A man sits behind a hatch and counts the banknotes the father gives him, then gives the father some other banknotes, and we leave. That evening the mother makes an omelette with ham and potatoes in the communal kitchen. That evening the mother and father drink wine from the cup I usually have soup in, and I get a fizzy drink.

There are no other children here. In the daytime I go into the street to find empty cigarette packets people have thrown away. They're free. They cost nothing. Grown-ups just toss them when they're empty. Chesterfields have gold writing on them. John Player Special as well. I like the red Winstons, the hard, blue Pall Mall packets. Occasionally I pretend the packets are people who can walk and talk, kiss, fly even, so they can just leave here, float off and fly, fly away. I take care of the empty cigarette packets, play with them, set them up on the roof terrace where the women hang up the laundry. I pretend they're people, sons and daughters, aunts and uncles and grandmothers.

The father asks if I want to come along to visit some friends. The mother is tired, she just wants to lie in bed. We go through a park with children cycling in groups. We arrive at another hotel. We knock on a door, it opens and we enter a small room. There are lots of men there, all with the same type of beard as the father. I sit on top of a bunkbed listening to what they talk about. My eyes sting from all the smoke. The father looks up at me now and again and asks if I'm all right. I nod. Someone gives me sweets. Everything is dangerous, I understand that. On the way home I ask the father to tell me what he and the other men were talking about, to explain what I didn't understand. He answers. The father looks straight at me and answers.

The hotel is full of other people waiting. Shadowy creatures who steal around in the darkness, who sit behind doors, on narrow beds with their sorrows, bottles, small radios and cassette players. I hear all the sounds. I move around like a ghost and play with my cigarette packets. They're superheroes, cars, sons and daughters. I walk up every floor and lie down on the roof terrace when it's sunny. I close my eyes. I hear banging, music, shouting, crying on occasion. Some people have been here a long time, others have only arrived, just like us. Down in the communal kitchen the other women laugh at the mother. The day we arrived she asked if there was a porter who could carry her suitcase. She stood at the reception gaping. It says hotel on the sign, she said. Now they make fun of her, the other women who live here. Call her *Madam*. Spit in the soups she makes when she's not looking. Then she breaks down upstairs, in our room. Curses the other women, the hotel, the father. Wants to sleep.

The women are also waiting. Some of them are here with their husbands, who sit behind the doors and listen to the radio, smoke and wait. They come from lots of different countries. I think they talk strangely, but they also sound nice, many of them. I don't say that to my mother. Other women live here on their own. They go out at night, wearing makeup, in beautiful, tight-fitting clothes. The father likes one of them, by the name of Rakel, I can see that, the mother can see that, and I make up my mind to hate her. But Rakel is often kind to me. Sometimes I'm outside playing on the pavement when she comes strolling along in the morning. I count cars. How many blue, green, red ones there are. She walks slowly towards the hotel, her shoes dangling in her hands, sits down next to me, lights a cigarette, stretches out like a cat and asks how it's going, if I'm hungry and want an apple, if I'd like her empty cigarette packet when she's finished, it's foreign, she just got it from a friend who travels abroad. Rakel strokes my hair. Says she has a daughter too, but she's grown-up, and then she doesn't say any more. She's a whore, the mother says. A wicked whore. She undresses with the door ajar so men will peer in at her. Have you seen the size of the tiny knickers she wears? She hangs them out to dry so everyone can see. Even the children, the mother says. But there are no other children but me. I'm the only one who sees the tiny knickers. I'm the only one who sees the father in the corridors at night, when he thinks I'm asleep and dreaming and I don't hear his shuffling or the bangs in the street or the car doors that open and close or the sound of men in boots and heavy shoes thundering up the stairs. I'm learning. The men are always coming to get someone. This is the deepest corner of the nightmare. The sentences where someone is being taken away, someone is taken away, where I can tell by the sound of the boots that someone is going to be taken away and never come back again, while the father thinks I'm lying asleep with the mother, and he sneaks into Rakel's tiny room.

Rakel teaches the father to listen. I hear them breathing at night. First him, then her. And then they listen to songs with the sound way down low so as not to wake the mother or me. But the father gets her pills from someone he knows, so he and Rakel can turn up the volume a little, and then I walk towards the sound, put my ear against the door and learn all kinds of new words. Rakel hums. Rakel with the tiny knickers is a siren. Who does that make the father? The next morning the mother gets up on the wrong side of bed, but the father has managed to find some slices of ham. We share the bread we have left and half an apple and squeeze what we can from the tea bag. Afterwards we listen to the radio with the cassette player the father has borrowed from someone. Silly quiz shows, interviews with footballers, and then the father puts in a cassette someone has given him. It's Rakel, the one with the tiny knickers. Even the mother knows that, but we have nothing else to listen to.

There are lots of single men here too. They have it the toughest. No country wants to take in single men. They just have to wait. Often they have to wait much longer than we do, the father tells the mother when he wants to console her. Now and again the father goes away, up to the delta north of the capital to help someone with something, then he returns with foreign money. The mother makes beef stew with potatoes and carrots. Chicken casserole with peas and potatoes. The mother gets a pair of canvas shoes and a second-hand dress. I'm not allowed to tell anyone it's second-hand, but who would I tell? I get an ice lolly and watch the children cycling in the park. The father holds the mother's hand. Ruffles my hair and says we should be glad that we're a family. The mother rests her head on his shoulder. Do I notice things are changing? I hope so. The father looks straight at me, tells me about the founding father this park is named after. Afterwards he tells me about other founding fathers. Every one of them was educated abroad, in Europe, he says. England, Germany and France. Then they returned here, with ideas, ground-breaking ideas about freedom, liberation and independence. I want to go to France, the mother says. I hope France takes us in. The people there are so elegant.

When I reach this point in the story, time begins to collapse. I sit looking at the painting of the snout of the small dog, in a museum in a big city. The boy is stroking my back, telling me to take my time, to breathe slowly and deeply, in and out. I don't know what's the matter with me, I say. But actually I do. It's time collapsing, tumbling down, breaking into pieces and lying strewn at my feet. I'm a woman who's obsessed with the past. But also a child who's obsessed with the future. A cross-eyed, dizzy child.

Later later later I'm an adult. A middle-aged woman in a green jumper, who has a job, who lives with someone they love, who takes the dog for walks. At the weekends I sit in the apartment looking out at the seaward approach to the city I live in. On my lap a book, a magazine. At the weekends I listen to music and drink a lot of coffee. But life drags on, somehow. It's viscous when I get up in the mornings, throw on some clothes and go outside to let the dog loose in the copse behind the apartment block. My legs are heavy, my breathing laboured and shallow. I go see a woman. She asks questions. I answer as best I can. Once, I start to cry while telling her about a documentary I saw about a famous footballer. He's from the same city I lived in as a child, at the hotel. I decide to tell the woman about everything I saw. The heavy eyelids. The smoke drifting in the rooms where I sit listening to the father and the other men. I make up my mind.

I'm going to talk, say everything that comes into my head. The woman asks if I'd like coffee, or water. I say: the age of my continent is the age of utopias. I say: we were founded by the Renaissance ideas of a golden age. I say: the Renaissance gave strength to the classical myths and transformed them, bringing the past to life and creating a humanistic dream of the future. I say: the discovery of the continent was an act of rape and rapes carry a demand for accountability. I say: epic plus evangelisation. I say: what was hope, yearning, struggle for the men of the Renaissance became for us – fatally – nostalgia. The woman says: who's *us*?

I talk. I drink water. I go quiet for a long time and stare out the window. Walk down a staircase. Step onto the street. I haven't eaten so I stop by a food court in a shopping centre. Later I go to the cinema and watch a movie. Can I tell the boy about this future too? About how I try to use my intelligence as a shield when I sit in the small room with the woman who asks *who's us*. Can I tell him about all the days to come after this pleasant visit to the big city, where he and I sit on a bench in one of the rooms of the museum, and I break down in front of a painting of a small dog, and the boy looks so tenderly at me, my first true love, so curious, so unafraid, so patient.

I make up my mind. I tell him about cramped rooms where lots of men sit smoking and talking. They look my way now and then, ask if I'm all right, if I'd like some water, a biscuit. I tell him about a broad, smooth face, full of disbelief. I tell him about a body tipping forwards, about a hole in the middle of a forehead. A wilderness of buildings and trees, endless saltpetre territory, rusty corrugated sheds and people crowding around to look at bodies lying on their backs, their arms outstretched under a grey, naked sky. The backs of a bunch of men in uniform, walking away. A jeep on a nearby ridge. I tell him about a bluish-black night roaming the streets with the father. What are we doing? Why am I with him? Where's the mother? A crooked tree by a river. The muzzle of a gun. The brown trouser legs on a body by the riverbank. A man lying on his stomach. But where's his head? *Don't look,* the father shouts in a very strange voice.

But I've already looked. Can I tell the boy about the future too? *Later later later* I'm getting ready for bed. He's standing in the bathroom brushing his teeth. It's a long time since that nice holiday to the capital, a long time since love was young, new and brave. I think he wants to leave me, and maybe that's why he brought up the nice holiday, to comfort me in advance. While tidying the kitchen after dinner, we remembered a song we hadn't heard for ages. So we looked it up and listened to it and sat in silence, each lost in our own thoughts. I think about the hotel. It's not unusual for me to do that but this particular evening I have the distinct feeling of being there. This abrupt glimpse is so precise, so surprising. Finding myself suddenly so close to the past is almost frightening. The tiny distance between the flash of this memory and the actual time I lived at the hotel causes me to wonder if I have become a ghost. Is it possible the little girl who lives there, tiptoeing down the hall with a cigarette packet in her hand, senses a breath of wind – distant, cutting – like a shiver or a gentle touch? *What was that?* she might think, before putting it out of her mind, because she is a child. But that night, while lying next to the boy who has fallen asleep, I can maybe answer. *It's me.* Is it possible to get so close to the memory that the person remembered perceives it? I hope so.

I make up my mind. I start to cry when I speak about the football star from the same city as I lived in as a child. The woman pours water into a glass and hands me a tissue. I'm ashamed. I stare across time at the small dog. I stare at my young love, wondering where the boy is now, if he's married, has children, if his hands still fidget the way they did when he heard me speak for the first time. Does he ever think of the hotel? I hope so.

People arrive here all the time. That's because other people disappear. I don't yet know what the verb *disappear* actually means. Yet the verb is quite common, as though the disappeared merely went off in a hurry to visit an aunt because she needed help with the house. But I'm learning. Prior to someone disappearing, there are lots of sounds. Sounds in the night. And afterwards, when we wake up in the morning, the doors to the rooms of the disappeared are open, as if the rooms were gawping. Then other people arrive. I see them go up the stairs with small bags, sports bags, a brown suitcase, a few plastic bags with clothes and shoes. They walk in through one of the open mouths and close the doors behind them. Best to leave them alone, the mother says. They could be dangerous. We don't know anything about them. They move around like shadows. But then I get to know them.

The shadows aren't shadows. They're real people but I only see them for moments at a time. They move slowly or swiftly down the halls on their way up or down the stairs. They make simple meals for themselves in the communal kitchen, which they take to their rooms, sit on the edge of the bed and eat. Some of them nod, almost imperceptibly, when they see me, as if they're not used to children, as if they're afraid I'm going to ask them something. But I don't say anything. I play my games. With cigarette packets. With everything I imagine seeing behind my eyelids when I squeeze my eyes closed in the sunshine and shake my head quickly. I learn some of the songs on the radio. Sometimes I hear music coming from the small rooms and I put my ear against the door and learn those songs too. It's a game. To remember many, many words.

The first time I hear the sounds I think it's someone playing at night. Maybe some children have arrived at the hotel, and they could become my friends? I hear thuds and footsteps, running and indistinct, distant voices. A little later it sounds like someone is letting off firecrackers, but by then the sounds are very far away and I'm not sure if I haven't dreamed the whole thing. But because the others living here are so quiet and nervous the following day, I ask the father what it was we actually heard. The father looks straight at me, lowers his voice.

Afterwards it's as though everything makes noise. I've never thought about it before, how it's never quiet, how silence might not exist. At night I hear the shadows climbing like demons. I picture them, hanging like bunches of grapes along the walls. I hear scratching. The mother lies sleeping with the sleeping mask she's made from a dress I've grown out of. The mother snores so much I have to put toilet paper in my ears. The room is dark, cut only by a sliver of light coming through a slit in the curtains. A knife of light.

There are no children here. Only grown-up shadow beings dragging their bodies up or down the stairs. They have all come from different parts of the continent. And here they wait. Time is empty, emptied. But everyone has a past. As I have a past. As the mother and father have a past. Some are engineering students. Some come from a port city where they had a cup of coffee every morning with a friend at the university cafeteria before heading to the auditoriums where the lectures were held. Some are primary school teachers, folk singers, poets and mechanics. Some have come here the same way we did. Over the mountains. Others have come in the boots of cars. Hidden in cardboard boxes, or under animal carcasses on a boat or in a truck. They close the doors of their rooms and sit on the edge of the bed to eat. Now and then they turn up the volume of their radios or cassette players. Travel back in time. Picture living rooms full of smoke and laughter. They all had hope, were young, were promising, and crossed a line. Then they were taken. Stopped by military patrols. Held prisoner in a football stadium. Locked up onboard a freighter used as a makeshift torture centre. I still don't know what torture is. But I'm learning. Abortions are caused by kicks and punches. Electricity is applied to gums, genitals, anuses.

Later later later I see how young they all are. They live at the heart of their present, with their own dreams and the dreams of their age intertwined. *Later later later* I am also a young adult with my heart in the middle of a present with a similar heart. Maybe then I understand what it means to be present, to be one with the life you live. It's around that time I meet the boy.

I dodge so many questions. I come to a halt, sound like a broken record. I want to know who you are, the boy says on one of the first nights. I've taken off my clothes, as has he. My flat is cold and cramped, but cosy. We've talked all night. Everyone that was here has gone home, one by one. My friends. His friends. And then the boy and I went on talking. It's dawn. Blue morning, the boy says, looking out the window. How old were you when you came here?

Time has crumbled. Pieces lie strewn at my feet. We stand looking at a painting. We've just slept together at the small guesthouse where we have a room. I break down. Did I learn that from the mother? What is it you can't say? the boy asks.

Later later later I'm a grown-up, a middle-aged woman in a green jumper. Time has collapsed. I think of it as *strewn*. Like seeds?

I'm a child at the hotel. I make friends with the shadows, everyone who has been taken, beaten, tortured, released and ended up here. And we're all *the lucky ones*. That's not easy to understand, at the start, but then I begin to understand. The ones who are alive, they're the lucky ones. The ones who die are the unlucky ones.

It's my birthday. The father has come from the delta with foreign banknotes and we eat cake, cheese and bread. I even get a drawing pad and some markers, which run out almost immediately. They were probably the cheapest. We eat. The small family we were. With a past, like everyone else. Do I think about everything I had to leave behind? I hope so. But how? But what do I do with the sorrow? *Later later later* I write down a line I come across in a poem. *I hope to be anchored in the eyes of those who saw me leave.* What does that mean? Was I taken away? I look at the boy. He asks me a question, looks at me, waits. But what is it I can't tell him? That I'm sick and melancholic? That I sink like a drowning man towards the veins of corals. That I cling to slow steps. That the person I was covers the person I am, like a leaf landing on itself, like a row of matchsticks struck at the same time. What does he actually want with my persistent and intimate attention?

Sometimes I think of the wall by the grandmother's house. That it remained behind when I left. I know it's silly to seek comfort in something like that. But I like to think the wall got to see all the things I didn't. I call them life holes. Everything that should have been mine, everything I had to abandon, forget. Now and again, when I can't sleep, I stroke and pat the empty desk I must have left behind at the nuns'. Picture it before I sleep, talk to it, comfort it. I do the same to my school uniform, to the bed I used to wet. And when I stroke, I learn to shift, to float like one surrendered. It's shameful in a way, an act of self-pity. But it's also pleasant, I feel I'm a constituent in a constellation. And then it's possible to imagine that maybe the desk might have missed me when suddenly I didn't show up one day.

Later later later I write a letter to the boy. We need a break, he told me, and travelled off alone someplace. I lie in bed, clothed, glowing. The night is slow and white. I'm so afraid. I've begun to pray to God again, I write. But my faith is incomplete, only works halfway. I picture flickering fluorescent tubes, my veins. I picture a clear, white eye. Always the same, heart-rending nonsense. As though I'm obliged to repeat myself. What is it I can't say? It's a horrible repertoire, not just the constellations of melancholy; desks, walls. There are also cut-off hands, smashed jaws and incantations. Blackening dust, unburied corpses. Pubic mounds, tufts of hair and entrails. I picture a man curling up like a bruise against the black sky. He disappears. Wakes up dead and soaking wet. He floats like a tattered leaf.

Later later later I study at a university. I live at the heart of my present. I've lots of good friends. We listen to good music, go to concerts, read books. I tell them that *once, when I was a child, before I came here* the mother brought me to the cinema to see a film about Medusa. We're good friends. Every morning, we meet for coffee in the cafeteria before going to the auditoriums where the lectures take place. I take notes. Kore is abducted. She's gathering flowers in a field and is abducted. I begin to tremble, my legs give way, like I'm fooling around. What is it I can't say? A wet body without a head by the riverbank. A chest cut open, full of silver fish. Nothing grows. Everything dries up. Kore. She's the one who's abducted and given a new name: Persephone.

Time is empty, emptied. We wait and wait. I'm bored, but then I see the mother divide up the last of the bread into three and I get the biggest piece, the only one with margarine on it, and then I feel ashamed. Run down the stairs and out onto the street. Walk around the block. Look for cigarette packets I don't have. Count cars, venture down one more block, then another. And there, near a playground, squeezed between two grey buildings, is a little church. Outside, a woman sits begging. Her hand is as brown and thin as a belt. She puts out her hand but then sees I'm a child and withdraws it. I walk inside. It takes time for my eyes to adjust to the dark. Scattered across the pews sit a few women sitting alone, their backs rounded. Jesus on the cross, emaciated and impaled. The Virgin too, with the son in her arms. I don't want to start crying so far from home. Do I refer to *the hotel* as *home*? I hope so. I sit down on the front pew and pray for forgiveness for being bored. I pray for forgiveness for my hunger. For the sleeplessness and for hating Rakel, even though she's always nice to me when she comes walking along in those beautiful, tight clothes that the father likes so much. I pray for forgiveness for having walked so far from the hotel without permission, for wanting to cry so far from home.

Time devours my memory. Tears it to pieces. Do I notice that things are changing? I hope so. I'm bored. The father tells me to go and play by myself. Maybe

I've been talking too much? There aren't many places to go so I sit outside in the hallway and listen. The mother and father talk about the desert, the mass graves and the people thrown in the sea with their bellies cut open so they won't float. They talk about young men and women falling from helicopters and military planes. *Later later later* it becomes a refrain, the young people falling. The father's eyes are blood-shot when I'm eventually allowed back in. I make myself very small, in a corner of the room, with my cigarette packets. The mother doesn't look at me but I look at her. Learn what her body looks like when she's trembling. Learn too what the father's body looks like when he's scared. When we cross through a park late at night. When we walk along the riverbank, when we meet a man who gives the father a gun. When we look at a pair of trouser legs, a body without a head, when the father yells at me. *Don't look.* But why was I brought along?

To learn. Sound plus non-sound. Night plus the knife of light. Open doors plus closed doors. Shadows plus shadows plus the child.

I'm learning. *Later later later*, like a refrain. I stand looking at a painting of a small dog in a museum in a big city with a boy I love. Then I break down, my legs go from under me and I must sit down. What are you learning? the boy asks. I'd like to know. I can't bring myself to say anything. I'm learning that my body behaves the same way as the mother's body when it trembles. I have the same eyes as the father when I'm afraid. My voice cracks. I feel my mouth turn strange and deceitful when I wish to speak. I don't trust my face. Am I the small dog in the painting? Am I really sinking? I'm ashamed. I want to say I'm a child learning all sorts of things, but in a country where the language is warped. I want to say that the torture centres have names like *Dignity*. I want to say that *decency* means to snitch. I want to say something about what happens to nouns when people fall from the sky like snowflakes, with their stomachs cut open. I'm twisted. A contorted child. An adult who is a hole, a tear.

I'm learning. Shadows plus shadows plus the child. I think about the falling bodies. They begin to haunt my dreams. The sea recurs. The seabed, the mountains and the snow falling from the sky recur. And the sky, in dream after dream. A sky in which the dead swim, splashing and playing above the desert sand like carefree children.

Sometimes the desert is a mass grave, a coffin. Sometimes the falling bodies are snowflakes descending into the sea. Sometimes the fish are the silver coffins of the sky and the desert a body falling through the centuries. I say the same thing, over and over again. See the same thing. Sometimes, in other dreams, I collapse, and with me the fish, the desert and the nights. Then everything disappears. Then it becomes bright and quiet and I'm woken because the mother drops a brush in the bathroom. She switches on the radio. I'm given bread for breakfast. Water. The father sits with his head in his hands. So much noise last night. But unclear sounds. Muffled, like when someone is struck with an iron bar. I think about Jesus. About the scene in the garden, the night they come to take him away. *Later later later* I hear a friend of the father recite poems by the poet who was found sprawled against a washing machine (or was it a stove?) in *the old country*. This time the mother is there too. We've been there before. It's a cold little place, maybe just the backroom of a house where someone has set up a few tables. Several people are reading aloud and singing that evening, standing atop bottle crates. The mother is sitting with red wine in a plastic glass listening with her eyes closed. How beautiful she is. How I love her. Afterwards I slip out, walk *home*, go into the small church and pray for forgiveness for not understanding the poems of the drowned poet, the man who floated like a garment. My God is hunger. My God is a plain. My God is a corpse. My God is no.

Do I notice time passing? That we're waiting and waiting? I hope so. It's my birthday. My dresses are becoming too short for me and the father gets hold of some money and buys a new one, which is a little long, and which I must wear all the time. My shoes hurt. I say nothing, try to walk barefoot as much as I can. In spring the mother cuts the tips off the shoes and tries to get me excited about my new sandals. I pretend to be glad and the mother is glad, less sad. One day Rakel brings me to her room and gives me a pair of trousers, but the mother makes me return them immediately.

Then my head begins to itch terribly. I walk around the halls with my hands buried in my hair and scratch and scratch. When we eat I try not to do it. I get sores, scabs. I pick at them until I bleed and wipe the blood on the dress and the mother notices and gives me a telling-off. She pulls me by the arm, into the little toilet we have. I can't deal with this, she yells to the father, who must come in and look at the crawling lice, at their eggs. He tells me to sit still. Show them to me. The eggs are white, slightly yellowish. The lice are brown, some almost black. The ones that have just sucked blood are reddish. When he squeezes them between two fingers, my blood oozes out.

The parents can't afford a lice comb. They can't afford lice treatment. The mother is ashamed, because lice are dirty. She goes into the little toilet with the father and asks him to check her head. But the father finds nothing. Not a single louse, not a single egg. Then she checks him. Nothing. But I'm covered in lice. I scratch. I can't sleep. The father says he can borrow a razor and some shaving foam from some of the men he knows, but the mother doesn't want me to go around with shaved head looking like a filthy, nit-infested child. We go together to a petrol station with a jam jar that the father fills with paraffin. It hardly costs anything. The father dips a rag in the jar and, little by little, rubs the paraffin over my scalp. It stings, burns, but I must not touch it. In the evening, he peels long flakes of skin from my scalp. We wait a few days, then do the same thing once more, until all the lice are dead. It burns so, when he peels off the skin. When I'm alone in the bathroom I try to look at the reflection of my scalp in the mirror because it hurts so much and I've been told not to touch it *under any circumstances*, because it might become inflamed, then it could get infected and we don't have any money to see a doctor or go to the hospital. It's a responsibility. When I itch, I sit on my hands until they're numb, until they feel like someone else's hands. My scalp is as red as meat, my skull throbs, a pounding feeling, wrapped in the smell of paraffin. I'm not allowed out of the room. No one can find out about this. My dreams are so strange, lots of horses, old horses kicking me in the stomach. I'm mortified.

The boy quotes a song. He does it so I'll understand he wants to be close to me, emotionally as well as physically. *If you lie on the ground in somebody's arms, you'll probably swallow some of their history.* He loves me. He loves the romantic poets he studies at the university that spring, the records he plays for me at night, when I can't sleep. I try to breathe deeply. He's so very kind, so very vulnerable, sitting there stroking my back, so very much on the outside *of what exactly*? He wants me to think about the beauty, inevitability and fusion in the sentence he's just quoted. We've talked about the nice trip to the big city, reminisced about sleeping together at the guesthouse. Perhaps he pictures us in that hard bed when he quotes the song. Perhaps it doesn't cross his mind that it's a floor in the song and not a bed. Perhaps he doesn't hear what I hear in the verb *swallow.*

At the hotel I make friends with those who sit in small rooms, the shadows that begin to call me, whispering and whistling at me as though I were a puppy. They want me to listen. Where they were cut. What scars they bear after which kinds of atrocities. Look at this finger, this hand, this back. Look at us, you who are still a girl, they say, and they ask me not to leave but sit with them a little longer, so they can finish their stories. I see large, white areas fall across their faces. I'm learning. The attitude of the torturer resembles that of the doctor, the surgeon. The prisoners are called plague-ridden, *the sick.* The illness is known as socialism, solidarity, community spirit, but also bread, work, education, dignity. The interrogators are mainly interested in making the prisoners commit treason. The prisoners must betray their own convictions. *Later later later* I learn that *the only transcendental theology is solidarity.* Maybe *learn* is the wrong word. *Remember* is better. By then I'm a grown woman who reads testimonies, reports by truth commissions and documents on forensic medicine. A grown woman in search of a childhood. *Learn. Remember.* Maybe it's the same word, when all is said and done.

Sometimes they're inconsolable, the shadows, just like the mother. Such faces, deformed and ashamed, buried in palms, are familiar to me. I hold out my child's hand. That is what I do when such faces appear to me. When a prisoner's hands and feet are tied together and their head is forced into a tub filled with urine, sewage or motor oil, it's called *the submarine.*

Rigoberto is sitting on the edge of the bed, crying along to a song as I push the door open. He's lost nearly all his hair, although he's only twenty-seven. That gesture – his hands running over his head – I'll see for the rest of my life. For the rest of my life, he'll call me *Chiquitita*. For the rest of my life, he'll drink from a bottle and say he no longer knows what he looks like. For the rest of my life, he'll call to me from one of the cracks. Whispers, whistles, makes *psst* sounds so the mother won't hear. *Chiquitita.* And I go to him.

Coco is sitting with a coarse blanket over his legs. I tell him about the church and he loans me a Bible. *God's abundant lovingkindness*, what does that mean? Something to do with protection, with compassion, with mercy. The light shines as though coming through a tear. Everything is dusty. When Coco speaks, angels flutter around the room. I see them but don't say anything. I learn to be completely silent. Nails from fingers and toes are removed with pliers. Likewise eyelashes. Jaws are smashed with blows from a hammer. Burns to the eyes, the testicles and vagina are caused by acid.

Julian trembles and trembles as he drinks spirits from a flaking tin cup. Then he trembles a little less. He collects stones, sand and hourglasses. He is one of the ones who has a window in his room. The light is nice, it looks as though white handkerchiefs were crossing the room in peaceful flight. Where do the similes come from? He's whistled to me, says he has the same dream over and over. People walk past him, lots of them, some slowly, others quickly, but their faces are always turned towards a wall. Then he's walking along a road that forks into two smaller roads. One bends to the left, towards a house enveloped in smoke, a boarding house of sorts. Behind the reception desk, a ruddy-cheeked woman sits, sneezing at short intervals. She's looking out at a small tree. Below the tree some pigeons peck at a rat on its back, flailing. But it's the cry of a child I hear, Julian says.

He gives me a stone, turns over the hourglass, asks if I can play chess, if I want to learn. I don't know how to play chess. But I want to learn. This is the queen, he says with his tattered hands and strokes my hair. He has a daughter too. A little older than me. But he doesn't know where she is. This is the king, he says. These are the bishops. But when he comes to the knight, he's not able to say the word *knight*, so I have to do it.

Coco loans me a Bible. I read about Jesus, that night in the garden, when they come for him. I remember my Italian doll son, who was taken from me one night. I'm ashamed I didn't wake up, didn't hear a sound, that I didn't see it coming. And now the son is gone. Now he's lying sprawled somewhere, abandoned and hollow. I become angry with myself, crumple up the cigarette packets, ruin the nicest things I have, then feel bad about it and smooth them out again. I tell Coco about the doll son. He says limbo is for children too, even for children made of plastic. Now he's the one who reaches out and touches my hair. Says he also has a daughter. And two boys. But he doesn't know where they are. I tell him in turn about the river by the grandmother's house. I tell him in turn about the lighthouse, the packs of stray dogs, the girls across the street with their long glasses and high heels and blurry cigarettes. Before they come for Jesus in the garden, he prays to his father to avoid the pain and suffering in store for him. He also asks Peter, James and John to sit with him while he prays, because he's in agony and close to breaking down in desperation. But the disciples fall asleep, not once but three times, before the Son of Man is arrested. Coco stares hard into space. And crucified, he says, carried around as a warning. It's said that the son of God *was hoisted onto a pole at Easter*. How old is the word *crosspiece*? I've really thought about it a lot, but I don't know if it's possible to forgive, *Chiquitita*.

Rigoberto is getting thinner and thinner, poor man. And his voice is so high-pitched, girlish almost, as he sits crying along to that song he listens to over and over. *Chiquitita, tell me what's wrong.* Lots of people here at the hotel laugh at him. Some behind his back but also many when Rigoberto passes them on the stairs with eyes downcast. *Later later later* I realise he's a young homosexual man who cries over soppy love songs. Is he changing in my mind? I hope not. One night, severely beaten, he slowly leans against a wall in the darkness as I stand in the hall covering my ears. He's ashamed when he sees me. Tries to hide something that can't be hidden. Maybe he wants to spare me, maybe spare himself. What happened? I ask in my equally high-pitched voice. He sits down in front of me with blood in his hair, busted lips, with one eye swollen, blue and watery, and says: nothing.

Rigoberto drinks. Julian drinks. Coco drinks. It's how they sleep. Sometimes I sit with them until they don't notice I'm there, then I leave, and hear clinking and rattling and the music is turned up or completely off. They want to shut down, flop onto their beds, emptied of thoughts, images, spectres, anything at all that moves. In their dreams they're scourged, beaten, found as skeletons in ditches on isolated roads out by an airfield somewhere. Then they wake up, sit bolt upright and hear me shuffling around the hotel, like a ghost, like a small dog sinking in a bog. I go down to the communal kitchen with them. They heat up tinned soup, which they promptly regurgitate. I wipe their mouths, reach out my hand, my arm. I am a lice-ridden ghost in a tattered old blue dress that's too big for me. They touch my face. My ears are as big as seashells, still I don't understand what they say. Nor do I know what they see when their fingers run through my tangled hair, but it's not me.

Later later later I call everything *my echoes. Later later later* everything comes to me like a paper plane landing softly at my feet. And my childhood unfolds and spreads over the voices like an even bigger voice. God, who doesn't help.

I see the Devil in a dream. He doesn't sleep, he suffers from insomnia, just like me. And just like me he drags his feet at night. He wanders like a revenant through the hallways of an empty school, a convent, the kind of school I once went to. At night I can hear him traipsing in the corridors in slouchy shuffling boots with jangling keys. Chains and shackles. The sounds penetrate the concrete walls. The city is quick to anger at night, like a pit of snakes. In a mould-green street, he beats a young man. He strikes a young woman with an iron bar in a yellow cell where the light is flickering. A lightbulb swings back and forth over a yellowing face. I hear many blows to a head. The lightbulb shines on the deepest part of my childhood, wipes out the child, erasing it when the light shatters in my head. For the rest of my life I hear echoes, refrains: disappearance, Marxism, the navy, cell, honour, decency, hood over the head, torture rack, officers' lounge, swarming in the dark. Thousands of snakes in a pit resembling the cities I lived in as a child. An aquarium where the Devil taps on the glass and calls to me. I'm motionless, past, an axolotl. I can't help but see what I see. I learn so many things. Electric shocks are administered to pregnant women with a tablespoon inserted into the vagina and up into the uterus to damage the foetus. Rats and other vermin are inserted into the prisoner's anus. *Chiquitita, tell me what's wrong.*

Do I miss the school, my friends, the grandmother? I hope so. Do I pray to Jesus for anything? Mostly I call upon the Virgin, his mother, the one I share a name with. In a painting in the church she sits embroidering, just a little girl busy with needlework. I look at her for a long time. Nobody's mother yet, the young virgin. No angels above her. No messenger from the one called God the Father, who is still a little god, padding around with no feet, with no body, because the desert hasn't begun to speak its language of generations and mass graves yet. I think a lot about God, even though He scares me. He existed before anything else existed. An impossible thought, really. God the Father, sonless, plopping onto the sand. Then he gets thirsty, turns slowly and digs a hole of nothing, because the God can only dig such things as the Self is made of. I think about God the Father, sitting up, looking at nothing, resting his elbow on nothing, yawning with his empty God mouth and finally saying everything that God says in the desert. I think about arithmetic. Desert plus silence plus language plus mass grave. And death plus daughters plus sons lying like sliced carobs in a corner of the desert.

Where do the similes come from? I wonder if God cares. If he has room for everything that exists, everything that resembles something else, or if he's too busy, and that's why I must recite my prayers to the son and the mother of the son. It doesn't take long to poke a hole in a person, says Rigoberto, says Coco, says Julian. A spear in the ribs. The metallic sound of teeth against an iron bar. The dull sound of nails against wood. A shrill sound. A discordant scream against the nail and a son bleeding to death, a friend bleeding to death, the friend who never comes home again, not even as a ghost. Julian's friend. Coco's friend. Rigoberto's friend. No kings fall on their knees for such sons. No wise men travel from the East on their donkeys. Nobody brings gifts. *The earth found him sleeping.* There's comfort in those words. He was my friend, Coco says, Julian says, Rigoberto says. My partner in a ditch by the roadside. His head had rolled a little further away. It lay between the yellow blades of grass, staring at the sky, as though he realised how big his dreams had been. Nearby, a thin, white horse stamps the ground. The sky above us, like an overturned stone. Someone places a wreath of ivy on my head so that I can transform into the implacable. *Later later later* when the boy I'm seeing moves in with me, that autumn when he begins studying ancient Greek dramas, I underline a sentence in one of his books: *who offends the gods by leaving corpses unburied.* Oh, mercy, let grass grow where I died.

The mother makes sure I get to eat, that I get the biggest crust of bread, the last knob of butter and the last half of the apple. She says she doesn't like people calling out to me. We don't know who these men are, she says. The father has travelled up to the delta to help somebody with something. He returns a few days later with a bag of meat and some foreign money that we take to the man with the long eyelashes and exchange. The mother brings me to the supermarket and we buy margarine, tea and a small block of cheese. I look at a packet of crayons for a long time. The mother strokes my hair and puts the packet under her jacket. Then she regrets it, places it back on the shelf and starts to cry. I hold out my hand. That evening we eat beef stew with carrots and potatoes. Name plus shadow equals shadow. In the church I talk to the mother of the son, the woman I share a name with. It's my birthday. She embroiders, sonless, immaculate. I pray. What do I pray for? Some more food. That the father comes back from visiting Rakel before the mother wakes up. That the mother won't sleep so much during the day, that she won't go down to the communal kitchen and return in tears. I pray for the grandmother and for the aunts and for the horse uncle, who I picture standing by a truck in grimy work trousers and a patterned knitted vest. I pray for the wall, for the stray dogs and the lighthouse. I pray to the mother of the son, the Mother of God, she who walks back and forth between the rooms of her father's house with the future in tow. She who dreams dreams at night that are too complicated, that a girl like her shouldn't dream because she doesn't know the meaning of all those words from the future: *theomorphism, theophany, incarnation, psyche, apocrypha.* I pray to her, she who does not think herself worthy of a future so grand, so glittering, dazzling and sorrowful. She who will become the mother of the son who has not yet been pierced, who has no broken feet, no gash or wound to his side, no blood on his forehead from the mocking crown of thorns. I pray to her, who whispers inside herself, because she too is a terrified little girl, who thinks her dreams are too beautiful, who feels conceited, who doesn't want to know what it all means: *ambivalence, transfiguration, holy mother,* because she's still just a little girl who is busy with sewing and embroidery. I pray to her who prays to be spared, like the son will pray to be spared. I sit in my small church, frightened, anxious and very tired. The nights are so long. The Devil shuffles round the hotel, his breath smells of mould, decay and bog. I pray and pray, there's so much I need. But then I feel guilty so I offer thanks instead. I grow terrified when I think: I don't know who I will be in the future, who I will become. Am I to walk into an empty tomb? Must I be sealed inside? Will I make a friend from Bethany? Will I become friends with Magdalene? Do we all have to have *Mari* in our names? I'm so hungry.

I try to take a deep breath. The boy strokes my back. Are we still sitting here? Can things not move on? Can't I just stand up and dry my eyes, clear my throat and turn away from the painting of the small sinking dog? *Later later later* I talk to a woman who asks me to search. That's all I do, I say.

But every so often they turn translucent, my internal landscapes, the movements blurred. A white plain, for example, with white, emaciated figures looking back at me. Maybe not white, exactly, but overexposed, as though too much light had entered. The repertoire is steadfast. My stomach hurts. I feel bloated, nauseous and dizzy. The weeks pass. I work. I'm a middle-aged woman in a green jumper. In the evenings I sit at home on the sofa and watch TV after eating a simple dinner. I live with someone I love, with a dog that is young at first and then grows old. I catch sight of a constellation: one rainy and windy autumn evening, a pair of glass doors, the way home from an insignificant job, the kind you have when you're young. Time passes, but it also does something else, I want to tell the boy who strokes my back.

We wait, the little family. You mustn't give up hope, a woman in an office says. Many countries take in families, prefer that to single men, they have it the toughest. She turns the pages in a file, mechanically, her eyes roving over it, not settling on the contents. She may as well have been peeling the apple she has next to the desk lamp. I'm so hungry, my eyes are also roving. File, lamp, window, apple, apple, apple. The father smiles, thanks the woman with a handshake. She wipes her hand on her jumper, looks uncomfortable, or maybe it's just that I need to pee, need to eat soon, we won't be *home* for so long. The father holds my hand as we walk out to where all the others waiting to see the woman sit, those who will soon see her turn the pages of the same file, see the desk lamp and the apple. But what about hope? What about everything I pray to the Virgin for when I sit on the church pew and look up at her, the mother of the son, absorbed in her sewing? The father holds my hand tightly. When we're here meeting the woman with the case file, he seems to change ever so slightly. Not much but a little. His speech becomes slower, softer. Afterwards, he needs time, I realise, because he's silent and uptight before gradually reverting to himself. Is he ashamed I've seen him this way, with his hand outstretched, desperate, subdued? I can't change any of this. It's a kind of insight.

We walk back to the hotel. The entire forty blocks. Past lots of toy stores. I pretend not to notice them, so the father won't feel bad about not having the money to buy toys. We pass a playground. Do I miss my friends? Do I still remember their names, the kinds of games we played? I hope so. We pass the church. Soon it will be Christmas. Three women stand outside singing in high-pitched quavering voices. They hand out cookies to the passers-by. The father and I stop to listen, wait until they offer us cookies. The father asks if he can have one more for the mother. One of the women asks if I'm looking forward to Christmas, if I've asked for anything special. I tell her I don't want anything, that I haven't thought about it, and ask if I can have another cookie.

A manger, shepherds, keeping watch, flock and angel. The mother has been crying for days, she cuddles me and says you're all I have. She's finally begun to touch me again, strokes my hair now the lice are gone, now I no longer smell of paraffin. I let her cuddle me. How I love her. She sleeps so fitfully. I hear her toss and turn at night. Make noises. And then she is quite still, like she's drowned, like a dress in water. Where do the similes come from?

I learn words like *host, census.* A woman is too old to be a mother yet becomes a mother. Someone else, the woman I share a name with, is too young yet also becomes a mother. I learn words like *temple, genealogy, sacrifice of thanksgiving.* I learn about the blessed child, dipped in a bowl of ointment. Blessed be your lice-infested, childish head, *Chiquitita.* Here are your gifts. A horseshoe, a spider, a ladybird, a pig, a dragon, a fish, a crane and a stork. Not your usual Christmas presents but that's fine.

Outside the church the women sing, high and quavering, as though they had always been old, of the past. Three voices blessing God the Father, he who protects the child forever. That is a vow. A horseshoe vow. A spider vow. The guarantee of the ladybird, and of the pig. The assurance of the dragon, the fish, the crane, the shining promise of the stork. I think about arithmetic. Life plus suffering plus salvation. But what's salvation? Some sort of window? A portal?

I line up my cigarette packets. The nicest at the front. Black and glossy ones with gold writing. But then I feel bad and put the crumpled ones first, the ones that are falling apart, the ones no one else would have kept.

What does grace mean? The small radio belonging to Coco plays Christmas carols. It snows in the songs. On the TV. Fake snow, bits of paper floating down. The mother of the child is only a little girl, too young to be a mother. And yet. A tree glitters in the sky. Terrified, she hears the Holy Spirit create new life. The body of the mother of the child, spread out like a map. What did it look like, the spirit, I want to ask, but Coco has fallen asleep, has thrown up and fallen asleep. I sit listening to the Christmas carol and think about God. The smell of a grown man's vomit, acrid, like ammonia. I picture a small rat by a huge eye. I see a battered man, only a boy really, and the mother of the child who puffs herself up like a fish, for the day will come when she stands by an empty tomb. Yes, that day will come. And it will burn like a furnace.

Christmas is coming. The mother has dressed up. The father has dressed up, and so have I, between them. The small candle that has almost burned all the way down becomes a magnificent star that will light up the firmament forever. The hard pieces of bread become wrapped, glittering gifts. Spider, horseshoe, ladybird and donkey. The king's child surrounded by wonderful gifts, foreign fragrances and brilliant garments. Everything is finer, more beautiful, more magnificent than you can imagine. It is, after all, the son of God the Father who has come down to mankind, for their salvation. But what does salvation mean? A way out? An escape shaft? The donkey stands at the edge of the manger in a display window. Long-eared, stubborn, loyal to the death.

That night I dream about the donkey. It speaks to me. No cape, no armour, no attempt to make a knight of me, the donkey says. I shall remain grey and uncovered. Look at me, the donkey says to the child lying in the manger. I will be the last thing you see. Remember me if you must, if you can, if you want. *Later later later* I think about that dream and ask myself: who was the donkey? Was it me? And in that case: who was *I*, who was I talking to?

I also dream about men in uniforms, men in silver-scaled cloaks of sand. I sleep fitfully, just beneath the surface of sleep, as it were. I see the child, orphaned, with no gifts, with no fragrances. I dream about a desert full of corpses, but then the corpses come alive as young people who light bonfires in the night and laugh, sing and kiss one another. I dream about ditches where headless bodies lie tossed like old chairs, washing machines and torn clothes. But then the clothes stand up and become young people who light bonfires in the night and laugh, sing and kiss one another. I dream about debt, about people sitting behind small counters who exchange banknotes for necklaces and other jewellery until there's no more to trade. I dream about a debt that must be paid. I dream that the child is the debt. That the child is the repayment.

The future closes around me like a claw. *Later later later* I consider them a kind of tribute to the future, these murders I must swallow in childhood.

I wake up. Christmas Day. The father has got hold of some cheese. I get two lovely hairclips wrapped in newspaper, but when I unwrap the present it's like I'm unwrapping the mother and the mother's tears. I wait until I'm alone to put in the clips; there are tiny drawings of rabbits on them. The star has appeared. The dreams have warned me. I've prayed to the son's mother, to the son, even to God the Father, who I find scary, absent, incomprehensible and mute. The mother cries so. The father strokes her back. Maybe she thought I wanted nicer gifts than the hairclips. Maybe I've been unreasonable, an unreasonable, demanding child.

A long time passes. We wait and wait and one day we are told to turn up at the office of the woman. The mother gets dressed up. The father gets dressed up. I wear a dress given to me by Rakel, one she's altered for me. We take a ticket with a number on it and wait for our turn. A long time passes. The father finds a bag of peanuts for me to eat; neither he nor the mother are hungry now. After sitting there almost all day, a man comes out to us and the few others still looking up at the board displaying numbers, and without looking anywhere in particular he says there won't be enough time today after all, we need to come back early in the morning. The next day the mother gets dressed up. The father too. I wear Rakel's dress. The woman welcomes us in, invites us to sit. Asks if I'd like an apple. Neither the mother nor father are hungry. She says she has good news. We're a small family and our wait will soon be over. She takes out a file, leafs through it and informs us about the journey, that we're leaving, that someone has finally accepted us. And then we leave. The mother and the father and me between them.

It's my first time at an airport. It's grey-white, almost empty. It's overcast, summer is turning to autumn. We've received some money, which we spent on winter clothes because it's cold where we're going. The mother is all dressed up. She's radiant. How I love her. The father in the background with the suitcases, and two women helping us with papers and permits.

It's my first time flying. I sit completely still as the aeroplane takes off. The father tells me to look out the window. It's beautiful. The city, the buildings, the big brown river and the delta. The cars and the people are so small from so high up that they're hardly real, then we fly through a cloud and I'm suddenly nauseous and must throw up. I'm wearing a green jumper. The flight attendant is kind and gives me an extra pillow, an extra toy, an extra carton of juice and I say thank you thank you thank you, but I'm nauseous and throw up the juice in a little paper bag and I feel so bad about that. It grows dark. I see nothing out of the little window. The mother sleeps with her mouth open. The father takes my hand, squeezes it, says things will be better now, things will be better, and then he falls asleep too. I can't sleep. I pretend to play with the toy I've been given and try not to think about the black sea below, about all the water we can disappear down into if we crash. But I must fall asleep all the same because I'm awoken by the aeroplane shaking as we fly through a cloud. The sky is bright, almost white, with a gilt-edged horizon, a fiery rim way off in the distance. Is that where we're going? Does God resemble a cloud or a rim? Some mountains appear far below, then large brown stretches of land, before a city slowly comes into view. I pretend to play with the toy I've been given and try not to think about what would happen if we crashed down in the city. My legs go to sleep and there's a tingling feeling, as if tens of thousands of lights were burning all the way down them, as if the new city was tickling me down there and we fly lower and lower and I'm scared and dread hitting the ground, hoping we don't die, hoping we survive, that we won't die now, not now that we finally, finally.

But it's fine. The aeroplane lands. Lots of people clap and I walk up the aisle with the mother ahead of me. Outside on the steps the air is fresh and cold. The mother says we must put our right foot on the ground first so that our stay in the new country, our life here, in the place we will be forever, will be a happy one.

It's always bright here in the summer, the father says, even at nighttime. He read that in a magazine on the aeroplane while the mother was sleeping with her mouth open, while my juice ended up in the paper bag, while I was sitting on the toilet trying to breathe properly. We wait for our luggage with lots of other people, ordinary people. I need to go to the toilet. My face is completely white, like that of a clown or an actor. My lips are red, as though I've been allowed to put on makeup like the mother does. I like it. I'm pretty when I'm sick.

3

Two women are at the airport to meet us. They're from the municipality where we're going to live. The sky stretches out, almost completely white, and we drive in a light brown van through the capital and further on to what *later later later* will be childhood's last stop. What time is it? There are hardly any cars on the road. I see the sea down to my right, containers, forklifts, moving back and forth like insects. Still hardly any cars when we turn off the motorway either and drive through the deserted city centre where *later later later* I will be an adolescent, drunk, smoking, searching, together with all the people who will become my friends, my gang, the tea-drinking, close-listening, novel-reading youths we become in a few short years. The women from the municipality pull up beside the block of flats where we will live, the last of four identical sugar cubes. They help the father unload the suitcases and carry the heaviest ones up the flights of stairs. When they unlock the door of the flat and show us in the mother begins to cry. The father strokes her on the back and I have to smile at the women from the municipality because they smile at me and assume the mother's tears are tears of joy, that she's happy, relieved and grateful now. There's a green sofa in the living room. We have a brown carpet, a sideboard, a small kitchen table and chairs and beds. A living room with a black and white TV, a sign outside the door with our surname on it, a nice, green letter box. The women from the municipality have made everything ready. The grown-ups drink coffee. There's a jug of cream on the table. I get cake. And squash. Watery squash. When the women leave, they hand the keys of the flat to the father, pat me on the head, then the father closes the door and we all collapse, as though we are a heap of stones tumbling to the ground. Where do the similes come from?

I've managed to stand up. The boy continues stroking my back but I can sense his utter relief, as if he's shaking off a terrible vision, and I want to tell him I can understand that, but I don't dare to say too much right now, just take deep breaths, shake it off as well. They are my visions, my stories, after all. He was the one who asked, repeatedly. And the feeling of shame – at being incomprehensible, repetitive and troublesome – suddenly lifts while at the same time I'm struck by a fleeting yet unequivocal acknowledgement that all this has something to do with duty. An obligation of some sort, but to what? You are a woman who's obsessed with the past, he's said. Maybe there's something unfinished within you, something abandoned, lost, just like that Italian puppet son that was taken from you. As though something was calling out to me, is that what he means?

I take a last look at the dog about to sink. Are you sure you want to go, the boy asks. Yes, I say. Where do you want to go? What do you want to do? Are you hungry? His hand is on its way into the shoulder bag containing the guidebook he bought before we left, in which he's underlined, circled and put asterisks next to everything he wants to see in this city with me. I feel so grown-up, suddenly. We've saved up to come here. We've been looking forward to visiting museums, going to bookshops, and record shops, maybe even buying clothes and going to cosy, little restaurants as though that were the most natural thing in the world for us to do, ordering wine and drinking nearly half the bottle while eating the delicious, warm bread the woman serves us in the wicker basket she's placed on the table. When the food arrives, he asks me if I regret having told him. No, I reply. I just don't know what you'll get out of it, I want to say, but instead I say: you have red wine stains on your teeth. But he persists. I've come to know him well. Even back then I knew he was like that. A person who perseveres. A person who can sit perfectly still for hours at a time in the reading room, concentrating, his nose buried in a book while diligently taking notes. I need constant breaks, have to eat an apple, have to drink yet another cup of coffee, but he just sits and sits. When he's finished reading, he'll find me in the cafeteria, and it seems to me he looks like he's just been for a swim, healthy and glowing. *Later later later*, when we've become grown-up, middle-aged people who have lived separate lives, he will call me up one Sunday, out of the blue, as they say, after many years, and will talk and talk about this time. And when I put down the phone, I'm grateful.

He doesn't give up. The food arrives. It tastes delicious, creamy and completely different than at home. Afterwards we walk out into the cool afternoon, hand in hand through the streets for a while, before we find a cosy little bar, squeezed into an alley, where they play one of his favourite records. I'm sorry for spoiling the visit to the museum, I say. Please, he says. I was the one who asked. I wanted to know. You're my girlfriend, aren't you, he says, looking at me sternly. I am. His girlfriend. And as I sit in the dim light with yet another glass of wine in my hand and watch him get up to go to the toilet – watch his thin arms and sinewy body slip gracefully round the tables towards the red door with all the stickers on it at the back of the premises – I feel joy within, a feeling I try to hold onto tightly, and not drive away with my customary guilt, this irksome shame about life, I think *later later later* when I relive that moment, that trip, that first love and everything that opens up within me, cautiously at first, but eventually bursting open, as though someone had carved open my stomach and out came what exactly?

There are lawns everywhere. Next to the block of flats where we live now, there's a small forest. And a ski jump. On the far side of the forest is a primary school where one day I'll be the new girl in class, with my dark hair and strange name. *Marisol*, named after the Virgin and the sun. That spring. The rows of garages below the block of flats and the spring light, the unfamiliarity of it all. I don't know any words yet. I'm going to start school in autumn. The women from the municipality came to collect us, and then we walked through the woods so I could see where I'm going to go to school. The mother and father find it odd that we don't drive and grumble to each other afterwards. The mother's feet are sore from walking on the dirt path. I think the forest is beautiful. A stream runs alongside the path. When we emerge from the forest, we see an empty gravel pitch with goals at either end but no nets. We walk across the schoolyard just as the bell rings, and suddenly there are children everywhere, children my age, younger, older. No uniforms. No nuns hovering over the ground with arms folded and eyes looking for something to disapprove of or someone to reprimand. There are so many sounds, so much noise and yelling. It looks like everyone is on holiday. I walk between the grown-ups. At the principal's office I smile almost all the time as he and the woman who will be my teacher try to teach me some simple phrases that they repeat more and more slowly before they switch to using their hands to point and smile too. How beautiful the mother is. How I love her. The father in the background, looking out at a tree and the bike rack.

I walk around the neighbourhood by myself. There are lots of other children here, blond, beautiful. Much more beautiful than me. The boys cycle in flocks. The girls have parked their bikes and play with a skipping rope. Everybody looks as me, as though through a crack. Sometimes, in bed at night, I make up my mind to wave to some of them the next day, say hello, use the very few words I've learned. The women from the municipality have bought a pink lamp for me, since I'm a girl. I like to sleep with the light on; I switch it on after the mother and father have said goodnight and closed the door. This is my room. This is where my dreams spread their wings at night and fill my sleep with wordless collisions. The blond children run into me, shout all sorts of things I don't understand while I make signs with my hands, smile at them and hope that that's enough, that they will like me. I awake feeling rested, but a stranger to myself.

It's beautiful here. Quiet. The spring is so nice. The summer too. June, July. The sun shines constantly on the warm tarmac I occasionally rest my cheek against, until the mother sees me from the bedroom window and calls me in with a high-pitched, piercing voice and asks if I'm stupid, if I want people to think we're primitive.

I hold on to something, and it's as though something wants to hold on to me too. That makes me feel a lightness of sorts when I walk through the forest, wandering between the anthills, trees and their rough roots. Before I'd only pictured *the forest* when the grandmother told me fairytales: 'Little Red Riding

Hood', 'Hansel and Gretel', 'Goldilocks', 'Snow White'. That's so long ago now. *Later later later*, when the boy and I move into our first rented flat together, around the time he's working on a paper about Dante's *Inferno,* I come across a sentence about the souls being tormented that I copy down: *Turning to make each side a shield for the other.* Maybe that's how I protect myself, with my body. The old life and the new, as I walk in the forest, the real forest. Am I already aware that summer that this is how it will be, forever? That I'll be someone who never goes back again? Do I think about my empty desk at the convent on the other side of the world? It's not empty, of course. Someone new will have joined the class ages ago, someone who lives, does their homework, raises their hand instead of me.

The mother is crying. She doesn't have very much to do. She leafs through some textbooks. The father in the background, sitting next to the cassette player he bought cheaply at a jumble sale that the women from the municipality took us to. It's Saturday. I've eaten a waffle, got a cardigan that has a strange odour, but that I become very fond of. The mother thinks it smells terrible in the school gym. She becomes sulky and sits outside on a bench and waits there. I ask if she wants me to sit beside her, but she motions for me to go in without saying anything. The women from the municipality smile at me and stroke my hair when I say a few words I've learned from the mother's textbook. Afterwards, when we arrive home, the father puts a cassette in the brand-new second-hand cassette player and sits in the same chair all afternoon and all evening, staring at the trees outside the block of flats. The mother makes tea and supper. We're the lucky ones. We have food. Bread and vegetables, apples in a basket in the middle of the kitchen table. She says grace, gives thanks, is moved when she does. The father cuts up an apple and I suck on the slices for a long time. I'm afraid the apples will disappear again, that the basket will be empty, that my mouth will just gobble them up and there won't be any left for the others.

Summer passes, very slowly. And it's this slowness I remember best. My mouth is dry and closed as I run up and down the staircases, in and out of the block of flats, up and down the grassy slope in the new trainers. But when someone catches sight of me, I slow down. I slink around the neighbourhood like a cat. The boys in a group on their bikes. The girls jumping with the skipping rope around their feet, ankles and thighs. Everybody looks at me as if through a crack. I sit down on the bench outside the flats. I walk down to the playground when no one else is there, go back and forth on the swings. Take a walk down to the shopping centre, cross the road and sit down on a low wall by the carpark. A thin man jogs past. The pretty girl who works in the newsagent's gets out of her boyfriend's silver-grey car wearing a T-shirt with an eagle on it.

The mother is busy in the kitchen. We're having guests. Other refugees, people like us, but who have lived here much longer. The mother makes coffee the way she's watched the women from the municipality do it. She says she wants to learn how things are done here. The guests are the same age as the parents. They have a son a little younger than me. He speaks a little strangely, haltingly. His head is big, almost as big as his father's. He doesn't particularly like me, because he barely looks in my direction. When the visitors have drunk enough coffee, the man opens a bottle of wine he and his wife brought along, and the boy and I are told to go and play. In my room he runs his hand over the pink lamp, over the chair, over the chest of drawers the women from the municipality have bought. He asks if I have comics or anything, but no.

The next time he visits with his parents, I've managed to get hold of some comics. The women from the municipality have driven us to some huge shops in their van and escorted us around inside while the mother and father were allowed to pick out clothing and shoes for us. I get a drawing set, as well as a doll I'm far too old to have, but I can't say that, so I smile, act grateful and stand looking at some comics for a long time hoping the women from the municipality will notice, which they do. But afterwards, when we get back to the flat, my mother scolds me. For looking for handouts. It's shameful enough having to go around here and be *given* things – smiling and mute as though we were all retarded – without me embarrassing us further. Sorry, I say, and something lodges crosswise in my chest, like a beam, while I turn the pages of the comics and look at the strange combinations of letters. One day I'll learn, I promise myself, one day I'll be able to say everything, I promise myself, if only this beam disappears, if only I can breathe properly.

These are for girls, says the son of the parents' friends when I show him the comics. Now there are some other children in my room as well. A boy playing with an ambulance and an older girl, maybe fourteen, pouting as she looks through a magazine she brought from home, with a blond-haired man with an earring on the cover. My room is tiny. I sit on the floor and pretend to read the girls' comics. The others leave me out when they speak to one another. The smell of smoke reaches all the way in here but I dare not open the window. There are lots of people out in the living room, people like us, refugees from our countries, all with sad stories like ours. They've all brought bottles of wine, which they open and pour into regular kitchen glasses because we've yet to get wineglasses. They are a luxury of sorts, which is still out of reach, I understand that after the guests have left, and the mother has got a glazed look in her eyes, both sad and angry, when she yells at the father that she hates it, that she can't fucking stand being the kind of person who doesn't have proper glasses.

At night no one is taken. Everyone sleeps. The father too. And the mother, I think, until we meet barefoot in the dark hallway of the new flat, among the flea market furniture with which the women from the municipality have furnished it. We meet in similar silhouettes and haze, each scratching at our invisibility.

The flat is filled with people like us. We also go to other flats, where people like us live, who've lived here for a long time, who speak the language, haltingly and stutteringly, but still. On our national day we travel to a city where there's a big party. As the evening wears on the police knock on the door because the singing has become too loud and neighbours have complained. I see the father in the background, eyes red. The mother with a glass of wine in her hand and a white, bright smile. She's dressed up, is so pretty, has such nice teeth, how I love her. I sit without language, mute, among the children of the parents' new grown-up friends. They exclude me. Or maybe they're just children who mostly think about themselves, and not too much about one another, about me. Maybe they're not doing it on purpose. Maybe I'm just demanding, an unreasonably demanding child. I envy them all the words they so casually use when they speak to one another. I understand very little of what they say, but have no choice, I must sit with them, because I'm also a child, I belong with them. We're often told to go off and play. We're given strict instructions. But after a while these afternoons and evenings begin to drift somehow, as though the alcohol also affects the walls, the chairs and the open doors. I become seasick from everything that seems to heave and sway when we children and the grown-ups start to get in each other's way, when the music starts up again, and the voices mingle and mingle. Some people dance with each other. Some dance alone. There's fizzy drinks and cake leftovers in the kitchen. Meat dishes and pastries from the homeland. Everything is shrouded in blue, lazy smoke. Then we hear a voice call out. One of the children is so good at playing the guitar that he always has to perform for the grown-ups. But also for us, so we lie down on the rug in the living room, tired and coughing from all the smoke that floats around us, between the grown-ups' stories and the heart-rending songs the boy performs. My ears are as big as shells. The father in the background, a glass in his hand. The mother, so beautiful as she rocks back and forth with eyes closed. And then, all the stories, the unbearable nostalgia, the wounds. How long do I sit there listening?

My ears are full of smoke. They are stories without end, because death lies just on the other side of a thin wall. A young man who looks like a scarecrow, untidy in appearance, thin and nervous. He tells of a *comrade* who never turned up when they'd agreed to meet. And that was it. Another man used to be a sailor. He looks like a bear. His voice is deep, as though booming from a mine, from a hole in the ground. It's his child who plays the guitar. The shy boy who closes his eyes when he sings. Then he needs to take a break, the boy, and talk turns to refugee camps, reception centres. The grown-ups compare sorrows and tell stories that resemble each other the way ballads do. We're lucky to have been moved into a flat straight away, we learn. Lots of people are sent to other, out-of-the-way places first. I hear about converted holiday camps, bunkbeds, fights, the frustrating language classes. Someone tells the mother how to receive extra payouts from the welfare office. Which doctors write prescriptions and sick notes. Insomnia and trembling come up. Nightmares and waking up over and over are mentioned. An older gentleman in a suit finds me in the kitchen, standing on a chair to take a clean glass from a cupboard high up. It's so late at night. My mouth is parched. He grabs my arm when I try to slip past him, tells me about his disability allowance, about time hardening, as though it were made of plaster. But it's as if he's looking at something other than me when he talks.

Rodriquez, *the Pole,* the death squads and the curfew. The torture. Severed hands. A tiny world, these living rooms. A world full of electric shocks to the genitals, of nails pulled out and eyelids damaged, hammers, smashed fingers and razor blades. The conversations stretch long into the night, like the sound of broken cassette tapes, deep, sluggish and slurred. A world of solidarity events, commemorations on the date of the coup, sad monologues and alcohol. The same expression on all the faces. The same refrains. The same noises, same cold, concrete walls and blows to the head. It's so late. The other children have fallen asleep, one by one. They lie scattered here and there in the flat we are visiting. I walk around with a glass of water in my hand. Check on my parents at regular intervals, to look for any signs. Are they leaving soon? How are we going to get home, it's not as if anyone can drive, can they? The father in the background, beside a slim woman. I'm ashamed of him. He looks so content, I think, but old too, even though he's only thirty-something. The mother shares amusing stories about the women from the municipality, mocks them, exaggerates. A man stares fixedly at me. He tells me how they nearly drowned him at the old offices of the communist youth organisation. Up and down into a barrel of dirty water. Like it was a fucking prank, he says, and falls apart in front of me, in a strange kitchen in the middle of the night. I reach out towards him. Pat him on the back. Remain sitting and hear the thin voice repeat the story. Under water. Over water. Like a prank. I'm so tired. Do I think about Julian? About Rigoberto and Coco? About Rakel, the woman with the tiny knickers hung to dry? I hope so.

Everything swirls inside me. It's so late. I don't know how we're going to get home. All the other children have fallen asleep. They lie strewn around, like jackets and shoes. I'm hungry. My eyes itch. I go into the living room. Some of the grown-ups have also fallen asleep. They lie curled up on the couch, among those still talking, shouting, smoking and drinking, who take no notice of them. *They took him too,* I hear the slim woman say to the father. No one sees me. He leans close to her with his cigarette. They beat him for six days before he was moved out to the countryside. He was locked up there for four weeks before being let out. He couldn't even walk his legs were in such bad shape. An ambassador got him out, on the condition that he would be deported immediately. And where is your husband now? The father asks, as softly as he can while the mother is in the toilet. Oh, the woman says. He found himself a blonde.

Was there no one to protect you? No one looking out for you? the boy asks, in the little bar where we drink red wine in the beautiful, big city we're on holiday in. The question makes me feel ashamed. As if someone roused me because I overslept. They did the best they could, I reply, more sharply than necessary.

Later that night we make love on the narrow bed in the guesthouse. He asks if it's OK and I say yes.

Afterwards I dream about bruises, about severed hands, marsh-like landscapes. *Screams that rake and cut the concrete walls of exile and nightmares.* That's how I'd put it if I could choose. But it sounds so pompous. A sentence like that would make me cry. And I must guard myself against that. I've cried enough today. So instead, as the city wakes to a new day, I say: what was your life like when you were eleven? He's so nice, this first love. Curious, brave. He makes room for me in his memories.

The summer passes slowly. But then it's over. I become the new girl in class. The one with the strange name. Marisol, after the Virgin and the sun. The mother comes with me on that first day of school, and she and I must stand in front of the class by the teacher's desk while she tells the other children about us, who we are. I've seen some of the pupils before. The group of boys. The girls who skip rope. The teacher pulls down the map of the world and points at the long, narrow country we come from, the mother and me. She hands me the pointer and, after looking at the mother – to make sure it's OK – I point at a speck that is the town I grew up in. I point at the capital and at the city where the hotel was, where we lived before this country took us in. The teacher explains to the class that we are *political refugees*, that we have had to flee from a mean dictator, and that we've been allowed to come here, *to our home*, to start a new life. And then she says they must be nice to me. They must make me feel welcome. How do I know that? How many words have I learned over the summer? Maybe I'm just making it up? Or maybe *later later later* the friends I'll soon meet will tell me about this day. I hope so.

The girls are kind to me. Sweet children with names like Anne-Lise Trine-Lise Inger-Lise. Every day we walk together through the forest, on the way to school, dawdling and messing around, and must always run the last part of the way to make it to class on time. I learn so many new words. *Stream, splash, waterproof trousers*. I'm the new girl. I draw maps and learn the names of municipalities, lakes, mountain ranges, glaciers and lots of kinds of trees, kinds of birds, and kinds of shoes you now need in the autumn and when it turns to winter.

The friends take me to the flats and the houses where they live with their parents. They demonstrate how to remove your shoes in the hall, show me the posters they have in their rooms, teach me how to walk a dog, not to be afraid of the dog, to jump in puddles when it rains, to close my eyes and stretch out my arms and let the rain hit your face, not to be afraid of the rain, to warm up with hot chocolate and a blanket in the homes of the kind parents who greet me with wide eyes, ask me things, and speak very slowly to me so I'll understand. I nod the same way the mother nods. Smile the same way the mother smiles. And the friends laugh a little. Maybe at me, but mostly with me, I think.

We walk into the forest, but we're not on the way to school. It's the weekend. The friends have things they want to show me. A forest track they called *the dangerous path* – not now but before, when they were children, when they were younger children. I'm not scared. It's just a game, it's not really dangerous. I often wake up refreshed. The forest smells good, smells strange but no longer all that strange. It's as if I'm holding on to something, but also as if something wants to hold on to me. I know I'm repeating myself but I can't explain it any better. It's like my body is being held. There's a sense of security in that. A kind of peace. I'm happy. The mother says I can just go to the breadbin and cut myself a slice of bread if I want.

I don't need to ask for half an apple, I can just take a whole one.

Soon winter will come, the friends say. It grows darker and darker each day. Now it's even dark when we walk through the forest in the mornings. I sit by the window in the classroom and watch the world brighten while we have maths. I learn that the darkness isn't dangerous for a child. That nothing horrible happens if you walk through the forest at dusk. That life isn't a frightening fairytale.

I enjoy it so much. I'm an ordinary child who plays with the friends. They look at me and call me *Mari*, because they think my name is weird. *Marisol*, nobody's called anything like that here. But when they only pronounce half my name, then it's not so weird any more. *Mari. Mari. Mari.* And that's how I say *goodbye* to the name. And get a new one. *Later later later* I think a lot about what's left of the child. Half the name when I'm an adult. When I'm a middle-aged woman in a green jumper, exhausted and hollow. There are so many cracks in life. Am I one of those who has desperately tried to close them? Or have I just sat down, melancholy and drained, and let everything defeat me? Hollow day yesterday. Hollow girl with wet hair in the new rain. Hollow, leafy autumn. Half a name, like a soldier, prepared for the winter that will come suddenly.

I've never seen snow. It arrives one day in late October, when I wake up, look out the window and everything outside is white and still. I run down the stairs and the friends stand like astronauts waiting for me in the fresh snow, and they point, explain and look up towards the falling snowflakes, big as tortoises as I stand staring at the sky for ages. It looks as if the whole world is on the verge of being covered in scraps of paper, as if God was dissatisfied and tore apart a page. I get proper winter shoes, a winter coat, mittens and a scarf. I'm a normal child with normal clothes and melting snow in my hair, with friends who teach me words like *slushy snow, sticky snow, powdery snow.* The friends teach me to make snow caves, snow angels, snowballs, snowmen. To walk on the ice down by the stream without falling in. They say that I must never – never ever – eat yellow snow. *That* is a rule.

One day one of the friends says *I think he's looking at you, I think he likes you.* The boy with the wet hair after gym class. The boy with the logo of the car dealership his father owns on his cap in sloping gold letters. The boy with the rectangular, blue Walkman in his hand, who sits on the grass watching the other boys playing football at lunch. The friend and I go down to her storage room to fetch the girls' bike that's been there all winter. It's just before Easter. The snow has begun to melt. The icicles hang long, dangerous and dripping from the gutters outside the classroom. And we remove our woolly tights in the class at lunchbreak, because it's much too warm for winter clothes now. Happiness slinks behind me. I really like that it does.

Later later later I visit a woman who I talk to. Initially she sits in a chair and takes notes. Allows me to speak and regards me with a steady gaze. I like that very much. I don't like eyes that wander, evade, look for a way out. I came here with my fear and I say: I thought my fear disappeared when I arrived here, that it evaporated among the friends, among the day-to-day at school, among the words I constantly learn, among the nice women from the municipality who arrange jobs for the mother and father. But then the fear returned, I say. Or maybe it had only been hiding. Maybe it was my own fault, that I just forgot about it and it grew big, snapping like an animal, hidden and caged. Like a hunger of some kind. Where do the similes come from? I tell her I don't know. Where do you think they come from? she asks. I reply that I look for similarities between ordinary and unusual things. Between a stuffed horse and a headless man. They share a silence, a seriousness, I say. Shame at being in such a state. What kind of state? she asks. Dead, I say. But you know that's not true, don't you? The dead are dead. They can't feel shame. No, I say. I don't know.

Happiness slinks behind me. Looking back, I try to forgive myself for losing sight of my fear. That I locked it up. That it hid away to grow in peace, so it could catch up with me *later later later*. But why do I need to forgive myself? I want to look upon the child with a merciful gaze. I need rest. I need sleep. I'm a child putting on trainers after months of winter boots. It feels easy, everything does. Easy to wake up, easy to play, to learn, to be the new friend of the friends. This is where mercy is found. In this ease, forgiveness is also to be found, the woman says. You must remember that.

The father receives his first pay packet, and the mother and I get almost identical dresses that we pose and dance in when the father comes home from work. The father gets his second pay packet, and we go to a restaurant in the capital. They order big slabs of meat, one for me too. I chew and chew. When he gets his third pay packet, the father asks if I want anything special for my birthday. The friends have beautiful posters in their rooms, glossy horses, lustrous, patient animals grazing, galloping, white and majestic, in herds, as though someone had caught a bunch of clouds and given them a plain to run on. I tell the father I want a horse and the parents laugh at this for such a long time that I start to laugh too. Then the father says: no, we're going to buy a car. That's your present.

I learn new words every day. *To run to kick to jump.* I fall in love with a blond boy. He looks at me as though through a crack. What does that mean? That I feel like a hole, like something that has split. *Mari.* Hollow gaze. Hollow gift. This life of mine, full of echoes. After I cycle home from school, I look up the word *boyfriend*, the word *crack*, the word *grow*. I like *to grow*. I want to write a diary and wish for a little, yellow book with a horse on the cover and a small lock that comes with a key. When she's in a good mood, the mother jokes that she knows where I hide the key, that you can't keep anything secret from a mother, that she can find a way to pick that silly lock anytime, if that's what it takes. I laugh with her. I hide the key in the shoe I wear. I write about the friends, about the boy, about a watch with a calculator that I want. I want a bike so I can cycle with the friends and not just sit on someone else's carrier or trot behind. One night when I can't sleep, they appear before me. Julian. Coco. Rigoberto. Rakel. They can't sleep either, they say, don't even know where they are, they say. It's three o'clock. The mother is asleep. The father too. Julian tells me about a group of young people in the area he grew up in, near the train station, in the heart of the capital city. Coco says the young people prepare a barricade as part of a nationwide demonstration against the dictator's regime planned later that day. Rigoberto says they have five used car tyres and a petrol bomb with them. Rakel says: when they spot a police patrol, they run away, and everyone manages to escape except an eighteen-year-old girl and her nineteen-year-old boyfriend. The patrol that apprehends them consists of three plainclothes policemen, five non-commissioned officers and seventeen soldiers.

I sit up in bed. I pray. First to Jesus, then to his mother. For nothing to happen to the young people who are caught. For them not to be beaten, for their clothes not to be doused in petrol, for them not to be set on fire. I give thanks as well. That we have food, that the boy – the one with the cap – likes me, and for the friends. Rakel puts her hair up in a ponytail. How beautiful she is. How I love her. Where are we? she asks. Coco says: the patrol's version of events is that the boy and girl stumble as they try to run away, causing the petrol bombs to ignite, and the boy and girl to ignite too. Julian says: after they're burned, the boy and girl are wrapped in blankets, thrown into a military vehicle and driven to a remote trail more than twenty kilometres away, where they're dumped in a ditch and left. Rigoberto says: the boy dies two weeks after *the incident.* Coco runs a hand over his thinning hair, says: the girl survives, but suffers burns on 65 per cent of her body. It's so late. I ask Julian Coco Rigoberto Rakel for some silence. The next day I learn – by chance – the word *teraph.*

During the Easter holidays, I think about Jesus a lot. On Good Friday I have to stay at home with the parents all day, even though the friends are all allowed outside to play as normal. We can't eat meat, because it's the body of the son of God, so the mother serves deep-fried fish and the father must turn off the cassette player or just play classical music, and he has none on cassette so it's quiet all day. In the evening, we watch a film about Jesus on the new colour TV the father has bought for us. I'm dreading it. *God's great lovingkindness.* What does that mean? Something to do with mercy, goodness? The son of God, the one who is born in a cave or a humble stable in the presence of three shepherds. Soon he'll baptise people, turn water into wine, ride on a donkey and die a horrible death on this very day. After death he'll descend to hell and on the third day ascend to God the Father to sit in glory by his side. He's a demigod, the son. A half god, a pierced son. He has the eyes of a god, eyes that can't see or be seen. And he has mortal eyes too, the kind that can easily be poked out with a stick. A chest of flesh and a chest of clouds. One hand with five fingers and a cat's paw. One foot with toes and toenails and one foot of breeze and swan feathers. The head is a man's but the heart is that of a puppy. I sit watching the film and see how he gobbles up scraps of meat, biscuits and bits of chicken with his wound. I can't help but see what I see, I tell the woman I visit to talk to, and the boy in the beautiful big city, who has just been woken by my nightmare. I tell it to myself as well. It's Easter, Good Friday. I dread the rest of the film. The son will be taken from the garden and the children who happen to be sleeping close to the garden will hear the sounds that are made when people are taken. And they'll remember the sounds, the children, and hear them for evermore. I dread this. I wish the son could avoid mutilation and death, the great struggle and the resurrection, to become king of the underworld and the judge of the dead. I wish he could just go on being a scrawny, carefree young man who works with wood.

Later later later I sit on a bench in the city where I'll live as an adult, where I'll become the middle-aged woman in the green jumper. I live with a person I love and a dog that is young at first and then grows old. When I carry him down steps, because he can't manage that type of exertion any longer, he looks at me intently. I see the serenity in his eyes. Concentrated, devoted. Is that like prayer? It's Easter. I think about Jesus a lot. About faith, sacrifice, love. *Later later later* I think a lot about how we become dependent on the objects we worship, because we expect some sort of external reward. But the truth – and goodness, and God – are unconcerned with our presence, with our desires, our expectations. *The desireless effort.* Whose words were those? I look at the dog who looks at me. Approaching the absolute, a total withdrawal. And yet: here I sit, across time. A woman turned inside out, seeking mercy, so that the distance between the one who writes and what is written can be nullified. In the middle of the film the mother fetches some grapes, another glass of wine. I wonder aloud why we can't eat meat on Good Friday. Isn't it bread that's the body of Jesus? And how is it the mother can drink the blood of the sacrificial lamb? She looks at me and says: don't act stupid. The father in the background with a cigarette in his hand. I dread the moment they come to take Jesus away. I dread the scourging, the exhaustion, the crown of thorns and the way he looks at me when he collapses under the weight of the heavy cross on the way to the hill where he'll drink vinegar and die. God sleeps in another room. What does that mean? That he's completely absent when they kill his son over and over again? Or is it called *invisible*?

I walk through the forest with the friends. They've been on Easter holidays and talk about what they experienced, saw and heard. For me every single story is full of blank spaces, words that have no meaning, not until I remember them and look them up in the dictionary. Only then do the stories become whole stories. Then I understand this business of *ski trail, archipelago, orienteering* and *coltsfoot.* I don't say very much yet, I listen for the most part. I think about Jesus a lot. Ludicrous, really.

The father starts work long before the sun comes up. At half-past five his colleague is waiting in a truck by the garages for the father to come out of the block of flats with his gloves and steel-toed shoes on. The mother is working too, finally. But it's a different type of work. She cleans other people's floors, other people's kitchens. I'm not allowed to mention this to anyone. That's how the mother creates a secret for me, which it's my job to keep. She's ashamed. She often cries in the early evenings. Because her friends don't write letters, because no one asks *how's Europe?* She shows me her hands, red, worn out from all the washing. It's my job to make her feel better, not so sad. I put my head on her shoulder and say I can be the friend. I can be the letters.

I get an old bike from a kind old lady who sees me trotting behind the friends and feels sorry for me. I get vouchers to the swimming pool from the women from the municipality. I get a pair of waterproof trousers from a mother of one the friends, when I turn up in jeans one day they invite me to go mushroom picking. I get sandwiches from the friends when we go on an excursion to a museum in the city and the mother hasn't made me anything to eat because she has a lot on her mind and wasn't aware it was normal to make a packed lunch. I get and get. But the mother cries, so I'm careful not to mention that I'm getting so much. I need to hide my happiness from her or at least make it a bit smaller. So I say that the friends are kind of dumb too, that the grass tickles, that I too think it rains too much and that it gets dark too early in the evenings. There are different types of crying. The usual. The type you can be distracted from. And the persistent type: the mother's monumental, exhausting bouts. It's important she doesn't become so unhappy. That she doesn't have time to miss things too much, think too much, be allowed to feel too much that she's just a little spic who doesn't speak the language, who doesn't understand even the simplest things she's asked when she's paying at the checkout in the shop, when she stands with a stiff smile of embarrassment in front of the lady of the house where she's cleaning, and is told to dust properly behind the cabinets as well but, the word *cabinets cabinets cabinets*, she just smiles and nods and doesn't know, has no idea about *cabinets cabinets cabinets*, which are no doubt important, and she doesn't know shit.

I was the one who asked, the boy says. Outside, we can hear the city stir, the city where we're spending our holiday. We've saved up, worked unusual summer jobs, even managed to put aside a little of our student grants for the trip. We've packed our bags, brought along books, because we're the type who read, voraciously and self-consciously. *Later later later* I find one of the books in a forgotten box in the attic. On the first page he's written the date, the name of the city and the sentence: *We're extremely in love, we're going to eat and read and become extremely smart.* I look at him and wonder if I love him, if this is how love feels. But really I know, it's only my own insecurity, my fear of making a mistake, that makes me ask the question. The shame of life. Only in retrospect does the love shine through. Actually, no. It shone that morning, but I didn't see it. I was a part of the light.

He gets out of bed and opens the window on the beautiful city we've travelled to. I stretch. He picks up a T-shirt, socks and underpants and goes across the hall to shower. When he returns, he kisses me and says how much he's looking forward to this day. He reaches into the bag for the travel guide and tosses it to me. He gets dressed. I look at everything we've circled and underlined. A graveyard. The house of a famous author. The large park where we bathe in the lake, and a second-hand shop where we come across a rail of leather jackets. He gets a black one and I buy one in lightbrown, very much like the jacket the mother has on in a photograph from when I was a baby. I look at myself in the mirror. Time swirls, coiling around my limbs like a snake. I have the mother's lips. Her nose. Her hands. The song that made Rigoberto cry, the song he played over and over in his room when he fell apart, comes from a small, broken speaker. I hear someone call to me. *Psst, Chiquitita.* The boy is standing by a rack of corduroy trousers. I'm dizzy. Out of breath. I look at myself in the mirror. See the mother in the mirror. I must check on the mother. I must check on the father. Look after them. They're so young. *Later later later* the mother will grow old and the father will grow old in the kitchen where they both sit listening to the same cassettes, year in, year out. It's as though they never stop waiting. Is the waiting for them like the fear is for me? Did they think they were finished with it? There they are. Celebrating birthdays, stuttering, submissive and grateful in a block of flats in a country that remains strange and unfamiliar. With a language that is friendly, but harsh. With winters that are white and quiet, but harsh. With jobs that harden and turn grey as one day drifts into the next. Memory can be greedy and demanding. It's confrontational, insistent. Sit down, the father says, on the day some of his former colleagues are found decapitated in a ditch. He sits with a letter in his hands, is communicative, then he collapses, soaking wet and sinking like a dress when I reach out my hand to console him. We're the lucky ones. We have food. It's safe here. The father needs to go to work. The father is not *grieving.* He has an all right job. The mother has an all right job. She cleans floors.

Like a repository, the new girl.

The friends are away on summer holidays. We can't afford that, but maybe next year. I walk in the forest alone and meet a girl there, not one I know, but I know who she is, she's in a different class in the same year. We just stand looking at each other for a while, and then she shows me a small treehouse her brother and some friends have made. She lives in one of the other blocks of flats with her mother. The brother is much older. He moved out last year and she took over his room, which looks out over the garages. He lives in a block down by the shopping centre now. We pay a visit to the brother in the afternoon. He's kind, good-natured, he looks like Santa Claus, but without the beard. We get cola in big glasses that he dries with his sleeve. We get some magazines with pictures of pop stars in them. On the cover of one of them there's a very nice-looking boy with long hair; he's wearing earrings and makeup just like a woman. It looks nice. We go home to eat dinner but agree to meet as soon as we've eaten. Back in the forest again. The new friend asks me which subjects I like, how long I've lived here, if I'm in love with anyone. She's very frank, stares straight at me and I like that. I don't like eyes that look away. I like people who see. I try to answer using the newest words I've learned. I weave them into the sentences I make and hope the friend doesn't notice they're completely new and untested. She's patient with me, helps me with the pronunciation when it's wrong. She says I have such beautiful dark hair, and I feel like telling her about the lice eggs, the paraffin and the scaly patches of skin I peeled off at night when I couldn't sleep, when my scalp was burning. But it sounds so coarse. It would be unsettling for her, I think and feel ashamed, because one day she makes such a face when I say the word *torture*. I apologise straight away but by then she's already hopped across a stream and is trying to teach me where to step so I don't splash in the water and get my feet soaked. Over the winter we'll become best friends and when the snow starts to fall again, she'll loan me an old pair of skis that belonged to her brother or mother, take me to the top of the hill next to the flats and tell me I don't need to be afraid, that she'll teach me how to straighten out the awkward sticks I have for legs, that she thinks it's nice that I've come, that the mother talks funny, but that I hardly do at all any more. And I understand almost everything she says. It's a joy beyond compare. I'm a child in just the same way she's a child, a completely ordinary one. She doesn't go on holidays, because her mother can't afford to take them either. She's so frank. Isn't ashamed. She wears red and green jumpers, just like me and, although she often makes a face when I answer, she keeps asking me things. Why did you come here? Why are you here? Why do they kill people in your country? What's the point? I answer that last night I dreamed about kissing one of the boys in my class, the one who looks at me as though through a crack. I answer that no one has come to fetch the mother's tears, that I looked up the word *decapitation*. The friend replies that she's never dreamed of kissing a boy, that she doesn't understand this business about the tears, she has never heard of anyone being decapitated. Is that really possible?

I wake up early and am afraid. But then I see I am here, that I live here now, and then the fear abates, as though it was just passing by and didn't notice me. It's almost six o'clock. I heard the father hurry down the stairs. It's beginning to get light. The sound of birdsong increases. It's spring. It's spring and then it's summer. Just before school is due to start again, the friends come home from their holidays. One of them has been abroad and sent a postcard, she says, a postcard that doesn't arrive until long after we've started the last year of primary school. I know so many words now. The most beautiful word is *us*. I relish the word like a hard-boiled sweet. Happiness comes padding behind me. We sit in our bedrooms, below posters of horses, and dream about the future, about kissing at the school dance, about dancing with the sweetest boys to the sweetest songs on the radio. We dream about what we'll be when we grow up. An author, an explorer, maybe a policewoman. I'm going to own lots of horses. Wonderful, silent animals. Happiness. Is that what's holding on to me? I walk in the forest with my friends. *Us*. I have a little past here now. I glow within. I belong to this forest. These paths have become mine. My name is written on a peg outside the classroom alongside the other names. The little past. I stroke it like a puppy. I recreate the memories into a pair of legs, a pair of hands and dresses so I can jump rope with the others in the class.

The friends say *goodbye* to me outside the block of flats. I know almost all the words now. This is where I live. With the mother and the father. And soon it will be winter again. I'm looking forward to that.

Bergen, Aug.–Nov. 2022

Also by Pedro Carmona-Alvarez

The Weather Changed, Summer Came and so on, translated by Diane Oatley, Seagull Books

Also translated by Seán Kinsella

Everything Like Before, Kjell Askildsen, Archipelago Books

The Man Who Loved Siberia, Roy Jacobsen & Anneliese Pitz, MacLehose Press

The Heirs of the Arctic, Aslak Nore, MacLehose Press

The Afghans, Åsne Seierstad, Virago

Killing Moon, Jo Nesbø, Penguin Random House

Also available and forthcoming from Akoya

You Glow in the Dark, Liliana Colanzi, translated by Chris Andrews

My Clavicle: And Other Massive Misalignments, Marta Sanz, translated by Katie King

they, Helle Helle, translated by Martin Aitken

Things That Go Unspoken, Antonella Lattanzi, translated by Jamie Richards

Book of Wills, compiled by Reem Ghanayem

Horses, Jake Skeets

The Oldest Bitch Alive, Morgan Day

Global Sex: What Sex Workers Know About Love and Capitalism, Sino Plambech, translated by Michael Favala Goldman

Mother, Marina Perezagua, translated by Robin Myers

Gravity, Ada d'Adamo, translated by Alex Valente

The Wilderness, Ayşegül Savaş

Chinese Fish, Grace Yee

Hafni says, Helle Helle, translated by Martin Aitken

Glimmer: From the Outskirts of Greenland, Ilona Wiśniewska, translated by Kate Webster

Reading the Waves, Lidia Yuknavitch

The Possibility of Happiness, Anne Rabe, translated by Lizzy Kinch

North of the Winter Sun, Veronica Skotnes, translated by Diane Oatley

akoya

An Independent Publishing House

Akoya celebrates courageous, visionary
and innovative writing from
around the world.

We are a home for authors and
translators, not just their books.

Discover more from Akoya at

www.akoyapublishing.com

Akoya Publishing
222 Kensal Road, London, W10 5BN

First published in Norwegian as *Chiquitita*
by Kolon forlag

First published in the English language
by Akoya Publishing Ltd in 2026

Paperback ISBN 978-1-83675-007-9
Ebook ISBN 978-1-83675-017-8

MIX
Paper | Supporting responsible forestry
FSC® C013604
FSC www.fsc.org

NORLA
Norwegian Literature Abroad

Design by Holly Titchener
Text design by Phil Cleaver
Typeset in 10/13pt Egizio URW by Six Red Marbles UK, Thetford, Norfolk
Printed and bound in Lithuania by Balto print

1 3 5 7 9 10 8 6 4 2

A CIP record for this book is available from the British Library.

The authorised representative in the EEA is eucomply OÜ Pärnu mnt 139b-14 11317 Tallinn, Estonia.
hello@eucompliancepartner.com
+337 576 90241

akoyapublishing.com